Robert Harborough Sherard

A bartered honour

A Novel. Vol. 2

Robert Harborough Sherard

A bartered honour
A Novel. Vol. 2

ISBN/EAN: 9783337046101

Printed in Europe, USA, Canada, Australia, Japan

Cover: Foto ©Andreas Hilbeck / pixelio.de

More available books at **www.hansebooks.com**

A BARTERED HONOUR.

A Novel.

IN THREE VOLUMES.

BY

ROBERT HARBOROUGH SHERARD.

VOL. II.

Quae medicamenta non sanant, ferrum sanat,
Quae ferrum non sanat, ignis sanat.

HIPPOCRATES.

London:
REMINGTON AND CO.,
NEW BOND STREET, W.

1883.

CONTENTS.

A BARTERED HONOUR.

CHAPTER I.

JEALOUS? I DO NOT KNOW THAT WORD.

THE pension where Charles now pitched his camp, was not exactly in Sorrento, but lay about a quarter of an hour's walk, through the winding lanes, from the village. It was most beautifully situated in the midst of gardens and orange trees and lemon-trees, pomegranate and myrtle bushes. The upper floors all led out on to different large terraces overhung with the drooping vine. The house had been an old monastery, and had, after the tyrannic dissolution of the brotherhood by an arbitrary king, been sold to the family of the people who then kept it. It was built round three sides of a quaint old square, in the middle of which was a well of great depth and most delicious coolness. The open side faced the gardens which sloped down to the ridge of the sea wall, the sea shore being approached by a flight of steps, tunnelled out in the rock, similar to those which led to the Villa Dresda. Apart from the great beauty of its position, the terms of the place were very much more within the reach of Charles' purse than at the Villa Castiglione. He got a beautiful bedroom, opening on to the upper terrace, and full board for six and a half francs a day.

Truly, Italy is the land for poets, thought Charles, as he sat on the terrace, the evening of his first day at Sorrento, and saw the sun go down behind Ischia. The whole sky seemed aflame with rosy light, which was reflected in the grey blue sea, from the distant horizon as far as to the line of dazzling foam that lapped the purple shores of Ischia and Procida. The effect was truly marvellous. Colours of every kind lit up the sky. Clouds, purple, red, blue, green, clouds tinged at the borders of their snow white mantles with pink, orange, violet, and yellow, sailed slowly across the firmament like so many gorgeous fairies ushering Apollo to his rest, or welcoming the pale moon rising, accompanied by a few dim stars, behind the flaming cupola of Vesuvius. Then, as the light died out and the blush of evening gave place to the frowning darkness of night, and the moon reigned in the stead of the blazing sun, the scene discovered new beauties. The contrast of the sweet, soft, white light of the moon with the fierce, ominous, ruddy glare of Vesuvius ; the reflection of both these lights in the restless sea, the gleam of the pale light on the shining leaves of the lemon trees, the rippling of the waves on the shingle, the last notes of the late cicalas, the nightingale beginning her chant, the wind rustling in the forest-clad mountains behind, the melodious song of some home-wending muleteer, the faint, far off serenade of returning fishermen, the endless combinations of beauty and music, each spot in the whole vast panorama full of infinite grace and suggestion, presented together a picture the impersonation of beauty.

A cheese-monger from Cheapside, standing where Charles was, would have felt inspired, would have learnt that there are things beyond Cheddar, beauties superior to Chester, and that Stilton is not, and should not be, the ultimate dim Thule of man's aspirations.

Though within a stone's throw of the Villa Dresda, Charles could never muster courage enough to call again. He lacked the courage, though he earnestly desired to see Euphrosyne. He would often start from the hotel with the intention of going to the Villa, would reach the iron gates of the Baroness's gardens, would stand wistfully looking through the bars, and still could never bring himself to enter. His nervousness never came upon him until he had first reached the gate, and often he would return a hundred yards or so, and bracing himself up make his way once more to the Villa, but his courage would then again fail him, and he would return, dejected, to his abode.

It was not till he had been over a week at Sorrento that he met Euphrosyne again. He was lying one morning, with a Homer in his hand, on a grassy bank by the side of the main road to Massa, lazily watching the dancing flight of some radiant dragon flies, skimming the dusty road.

The Homer did not receive much attention, and who should blame its reader? The past is all very well when the present palls, but when all invites to enjoyment and ease the present should be enjoyed. What day-dreams passed through Charles's head as he gazed wistfully towards the sea, what emblems were suggested, what music faintly echoed in his mind? All the beauty of the world was there, and there only for Euphrosyne.

Euphrosyne was taking a walk alone in that direction, she passed Charles without being noticed although at the time his full eyes were fixed on her. He was thinking of her, she was there, but he did not notice her. It was not till she bowed to him that he started to his feet, with flushed cheeks, and with his hair in the wildest confusion. He did not seem to understand for a moment or two, then he laughed and gave her greeting.

"Excuse me, mademoiselle, I was dreaming, I think; I did not see you."

"You had your eyes on me," said Euphrosyne smiling.

"Yes, over there," said he, pointing to the skies of the horizon.

Euphrosyne looked at him, and paused. Then she said—

"Are you staying here? Is di Caserta here too?"

"Always di Caserta, always di Caserta," thought Charles. He answered that he thought the Duke was still at Naples, he had not seen him for more than a week. Then he asked timidly if he might walk a little way with her—he felt lonely he said.

She felt lonely she answered, he might walk with her. Why had he never called if he had been in Sorrento a week? She so much wanted to hear about di Caserta. What was this service he had done him?

"Nothing," answered Charles bitterly. "I lent him a little money. *Voilá tout.*"

"Did Arnolfo want money?" asked Euphrosyne. "How strange that he should have asked you. The Baroness would"—

"He did not ask me," said Charles, interrupting, "I lent it to him. He paid it back. That is the end."

They walked on in silence. At last Charles broke out—

"Why are you so interested in the Duke?"

Without a sign of hesitation, but with a little blush and a voice full of infinite tenderness, Euphrosyne answered—

"I love him."

There, he had it from her lips. It was finished, this dream of his. She was not of much worth, after all. His question had been indiscreet, but how indiscreet her answer. What would a love be worth that was proclaimed to strangers? Where was her modesty, her maidenly reserve?

Euphrosyne continued—

"You know what love is, do you not? You love Horace, you say."

"Bah!" said Charles, "Is that love? I may feel for him, that were he here to-day, a contemporary, I should admire him, and perhaps love him. The love for a memory, for a name, is not the same as the love for a living person. Do you understand me?"

"Hardly; I can fancy loving and hating a memory, a man of past ages, a name, as strongly as a man of to-day. I put Dante under my pillow and threw Voltaire into the fire when I was a child."

"And now are you no longer a child?"

"Ah, me! I fear not," said Euphrosyne sadly. "I love to think so, but they will not let me be one, I think. I must walk and not run. I may not sing now when my heart is full of pleasure. I must be quiet and reserved. Ah, no! I am no child."

"Is it quiet and reserved to tell a stranger whom you love?"

Euphrosyne was silent awhile, then she said—

"You asked me."

"I did, and I am sorry; there are things we had better not know. Delusions are sweet sometimes."

"Why should you be sorry?"

"Would you not be sorry if one day your lover told you that he loved another woman?"

"No; why, I should be glad. I think it makes people happy to love."

"Would it not make you jealous?"

"Jealous—I do not know that word. It is a word I do not understand."

Charles stopped, and looked her full in the eyes. There was a truth there, in its well of liquid light. They walked back.

"Tell me," said Euphrosyne, "what you mean; tell it to me over again."

"I said that there are things which men would rather never hear. There are dreams from which there should be no awaking. I was happy before you said what you did; I am not happy now."

"Do you not like Arnolfo?"

"Yes."

"Why then be angry with me for sharing your feeling towards him. Oh! he is noble, he is generous, he is beautiful."

"Your love is no uncommon one," said Charles with a short laugh. "Beauty and generosity soon find hearts to love them. I liked him for neither of these qualities."

"But you do like him, and this makes me happy."

After this Charles reverted no more to the subject. He talked to the girl of love and war, of heroes and heroines, of beauty and chivalry, of romance and pathos, and made her interested and pleased with him. When he left her at the gates of the Villa Dresda she put out her hand and said—

"You are very clever. I shall like you too. Good-bye."

Charles returned to his pension full of bitter and remorseful thoughts. The time he had spent with Euphrosyne had only served to feed the flame of his love. He did not understand her, that is certain. He did not understand the priceless value of the girl he loved. She was not the ordinary woman he took her for. He saw her only with the eyes of the body, he saw her only in the flesh. He had not known her long enough to learn that even if beauty did not claim her as favourite daughter, she would still be of women the most desirable. Like a miser gloating over the golden case of a casket, full of the most rare and beautiful pearls, without knowing its contents, he was taken by her form alone. And yet who, looking into her deep eyes, could not read the innocence, the purity, the childlike simplicity of her character. Yet, in spite of his ignorance of her full value, he loved her intensely. She was worth more than any man born could ever offer her.

He again returned to the thought that she admired the Duke as a wealthy man, as the descendant of a long line of glorious ancestors, and with this thought returned his regret. The regret brought with it perverseness, and, let it be said, he felt glad he had written to Dorothy as he had.

He entered the hotel, and spent the minutes before lunch in turning over the leaves of the visitors' book which lay in the hall, indulging in all kinds of speculations, suggested by the names therein. Amongst the names that occurred in the last year's register he came across the following :—

"JOHN MERTON AND LADY,
"San Francisco, U.S."

Suddenly it flashed across his mind that this was the name of the man who had betrayed his friend Lovell's friend. With pleasurable excitement, for he rejoiced at the chance of doing his friend, to whom he felt grateful for various kindness, a valuable service, he called a waiter, and pointing to the names, asked the man for information about those people.

The waiter replied that they were Americans, that they had stayed there a few weeks, that they had been very liberal to him, emphasising this latter, that they were travelling in Italy, and that they were, according to a letter the proprietor had that morning received, about to return to Sorrento, and finally that lunch was ready.

Charles took breakfast hastily, and spoke to the proprietor, who confirmed the waiter's statement, and added that Mr. and Mrs. Merton were expected in three or four days.

Charles walked straight to Sorrento, and, going to the telegraph station, sent the following message to Lovell :—

"Sorrento.

"DEAR LOVELL—

"A man called John Merton and a woman of the same name are expected here in a few days, at the Grande Sentinelle Hotel. Both Americans, and hailing from San Francisco.

"Yours,

"HAUBERK."

Late that evening he received the answer—

"Leipzic.

"DEAR HAUBERK—

"Eternal thanks for message. I leave for Naples to-night, on Bartholomew's track. If only I can see Esther.

"Yours most affectionately,

"HERBERT LOVELL."

In four days Charles received another telegram from his friend, from Rome, announcing his arrival there. About the time that he received the telegram Mr. John Merton and lady arrived at the Grande Sentinelle.

Charles went to Naples to meet Herbert, who arrived at about four in the afternoon by the express. The two friends were very glad to see each other. Herbert was especially pleased at seeing Charles. He was very much excited, and appeared wild and unsettled. The thought of seeing his dear friend, still dear though stained and dishonoured, again was uppermost in his mind. He kept appealing to Charles as they drove from Castellamare to Sorrento—

"Let me see her! let me see her! and then for Bartholomew."

CHAPTER II.

JOHN MERTON AND LADY.

THE carriage which they had taken at Castellamare (for it was too late to reach Sorrento by sea, and they had had to go round the bay by train as far as Castellamare and on by carriage) did not proceed fast enough for the impatient young American, who, as he approached nearer his destination, appeared to be burning with excitement, and continually urged the driver to lash his horses on. The beauties of one of the most picturesque drives in the world were thrown away upon him, not one of the manifold features of transcendent interest, which the landscape as well as the people must present to all who see Naples for the first time, elicited a single remark.

"Yes, it is beautiful I daresay," he would say, whenever Charles pointed out some beautiful view or place of interest. "But where is Esther? where is Esther?" As each of the villages which lie between Castellamare and Sorrento were approached, he would clutch Charles by the arm, and ask in a voice hoarse with excitement, "Is that Sorrento?" and when he heard how far it was still off would sink back peevishly in his seat, only to spring up again, and repeat, "Where is Esther? where is Esther?"

As they drew near the village he could hardly

restrain himself from jumping out of the carriage and running thither, but contented himself with shouting to the driver, in French, German, and English, to drive his horses faster. Charles, as he marked the hectic flush on the young man's cheek, and saw his nervous hands ball and loosing, and heard his breath coming and going in short spasmodic gasps, and saw his whole form quivering with excitement, felt that he must never permit him to see his enemy in such a state if he wished to prevent *murder!* He spoke to Lovell and bade him be calm, but all the answer he got was the same, "Where is Esther? where is Esther?"

At last the Grande Sentinelle was reached; it was seven o'clock, and they had done their drive in good time. At least so the driver remarked, pointing to his steaming and foam-covered horses.

Lovell tossed him some money, and bidding Charles "follow," shouted out as he entered the house, "Where is the proprietor?"

The man of the house approached, and asked him what he wanted.

Charles made him a sign, but the man did not notice it—the hall was dark.

Lovell said, in a voice quivering with excitement—

"You have here a Mrs. Merton; where is she?"

Charles repeated the sign.

The man said—

"La Signora Merton, with il Signor Merton, are in their apartments on the first floor. They do not dine at *table d'hôte.*"

Lovell tore upstairs, Charles after him, leaving the proprietor in amazement, thinking that surely some lunatic was at large.

"Be calm, be calm," said Charles, as he reached his friend, who was standing on the landing of the first floor.

"Calm I need be! Where is she? Where is she?" continued he. "By God, I will break down every door in the house but I will find her; and him, ah! him."

While he was yet speaking a door that led on to the landing was opened, and a waiter came out, saying, as he closed the door—

"Yes, Signora Merton, I will attend to your order. Did you say at six?"

The words were hardly out of the man's mouth, and before Charles could stop him, when with a cry that had little of human in it Herbert dashed at the door, thrust the waiter aside, burst the door rather than pushed it open, and rushed into the room. The room was dimly lighted. One solitary candle on the piano, at which a lady was playing, shed a feeble light, but by it could be discerned the figure of a man standing by the open window.

Herbert had taken all this in at a glance; he crossed the room and went up to the woman without a word, with his arms out, his dress in confusion, and tottering rather than walking.

The man, who had been startled by his entry, and who probably took him for a drunken guest of the pension, stepped in between them.

With a cry of rage Herbert leapt upon him, and

seizing him by the throat dashed him aside. The woman gave a startled cry and snatched up the candle, throwing its full light upon the intruder, and at the same time discovering her features. But Herbert was blinded and with a cry of "Esther, I have found you," threw his arms round her.

The man, who had recovered from Herbert's attack, jumped to the rescue, seized him by the collar, and dragged him away, saying—

"Are you mad, sir, or drunk?"

Herbert struggled and freed himself, and then for the first time looked at the man. The girl had run to the door, and was crying for help. Charles had entered the room and stood prepared to prevent further violence.

"Who are you, and what do you want?" said John Merton.

Herbert looked at him. The darkness of the room, lit now only by the dim light of the evening, prevented him from seeing the person's face. He said slowly, as if repeating something he had learnt by heart—

"You are tall, you are violent. You call yourself John Merton. You are a liar and a thief. I am Herbert Lovell, and you are Bartholomew."

The man laughed a merry laugh. Herbert continued, interposing himself between the door—

"It is not the time to laugh now. You have had more than three years for mirth. Your sorrows shall begin now. I know you. I know you as a villain and a thief. I have come to take Esther from you. I have come to punish you."

John Merton listened to him in the greatest amazement. Then he said—

"I hear by your accent that you are an American. You are probably drunk. You have played your nonsense long enough, and now you will leave my room. If you live in the house I shall come to you to-morrow for an explanation of this. You have insulted my sister."

"You lie," said Herbert; "you lie. Not your sister, your mistress! Bartholomew! Thief, embezzler, seducer, you see that I know you!"

"This is really getting too strong," said John Merton, who began to recognize that he was dealing not with a drunkard, but either with a lunatic or with somebody labouring under a strong delusion. "I do not know what you mean. My name is John Merton, not Bartholomew. The lady is my sister, Mildred Merton; and, here, I have had enough of this. Go and get something cooling to drink, and get out."

What Herbert might have done in his fury cannot be said had not the people of the house, aroused by Mildred's cries, come hurrying to the room with lights and dragged Herbert away, who was just commencing a second and more violent attack on the supposed Bartholomew.

"What is the matter?" said the proprietor of the establishment, who was, with two waiters, holding Lovell back.

There was plenty of light in the room now. Mildred had entered, and stood behind her brother, frightened and pale.

Herbert glanced at the Mertons. Instead of the villanous face of Bartholomew, he saw the fresh, cheerful face of a young man of about twenty, and, instead of Esther, a fair-haired girl, whose age her most jealous detractors could not have put higher than eighteen.

He stood looking at them, and they, with no less astonishment, at him. It was clear neither party had seen the other before. The proprietor, still clinging to Herbert, repeated his question. There was a long silence. Most of the *pensionnaires* had gathered together on the first landing, and were crowding their heads in at the door, anxious to learn what was the matter.

At last Herbert spoke. He had recovered his self-command, though he looked as if he could not understand the matter at all, an expression which by the way, was seated on the faces of all those present.

"It is a mistake," said he.

"Your hear that?" said John Merton, waving his hand to bid the proprietor release Herbert and leave the room. "It is a mistake. Ladies and gentlemen, there is no cause for alarm, and no reason why you should not return to your dinner."

Then, as the people went away, by no means satisfied at this *dénouement* of what had promised to be a tragic adventure, he closed the door, and going up to Herbert, who was leaning exhausted and as a man in a dream on Charles' arm, he said—

"Now, countryman, what was this mistake?"

But poor Herbert could not answer. Shame, wonder, and regret enforced silence in him. He stood for some time in the same position, looked at John Merton, then at his sister, and finally at Charles, who was as astonished as the rest. At last he said, addressing the latter—

"I think I had better go back to Leipzic," and with this he walked to the door.

"No, no," said Charles, interposing himself; "no, Herbert, you *must* explain yourself to this lady at least. You must see that."

"What is it all about?" said John Merton, addressing Charles.

"I hardly know myself. It appears my friend has lost a dear friend, a relation, I believe, who ran away from X—, in the States, with a person who assumed the name of John Merton. My friend has just come all the way from Saxony to meet you. He took you for the man, I suppose, in the dark, and the lady, your sister, for the lady."

"X—, in the States?" cried John and Mildred at the same time.

"Yes X—, in the States," said Herbert, who had somewhat recovered. "But I see it is a mistake. I am dazed and ashamed to-night, to-morrow, if you will let me, I will explain all. I can show you then that I had grounds for a mistake. I am truly sorry at what has happened. I hope the lady will forgive me. I think she will when she hears that I took her for," cried he bitterly, "the best friend I ever had—for an unhappy, unhappy woman."

"No, countryman," said John kindly, taking him by the hand, 'not to-morrow, to-night. Yet rest a little; you are tired and excited. Mildred, a chair for our countryman. Mildred, some brandy, quick. There, friend, sit down; and you, sir, kindly take a seat. You will tell us about it by-and-bye, and I think I can see something clear in this mystery. Mildred, do you remember Doctor Toogood?"

"Can I ever forget him, John?"

"Do you remember the bag and umbrella?"

"Of course."

"Then I think I can meet our countryman half-way in his explanation. Do you know, Mildred, that I think we must learn to forget our benefactor."

"Forget him! John, oh, never!"

"Forget him, if we would not think of him other than as an angel from heaven. I fear we were only the tools of a designing man. I fear we shall have to learn to forget him if we would not unsay the prayers we have said for him together, forget him before we recall the blessings our old mother spoke over him, forget him before we resolve to follow the last words, the last command, she gave us on her deathbed."

Herbert, who had listened to this conversation in a kind of stupified amazement, rose and said vaguely, "Then you are not Bartholomew?"

"No," said John Merton with a smile. "I understand your mistake now. I am afraid I know Bartholomew."

"Where? where is he?" cried Herbert, starting to his feet.

"I don't know. I met him at X— more than three years ago."

"How? as Bartholomew?"

"No, as Doctor Toogood."

"Tell me, tell me!" cried Herbert; "tell me all about it."

"Perhaps," said Charles, "as this is apparently a family matter, I had better retire?"

"Do you want your brother to go?" asked John Merton, addressing Herbert.

"Who?" asked Herbert.

"Your brother; are you not his brother?" said John, indicating Charles.

"No," answered Charles quickly, "certainly not, I am Charles Hauberk."

"No," said Herbert, with a glance of affection at his friend. "No, we are not brothers, we are good friends."

"I beg your pardon, gentlemen," said John, looking from one to the other, "I thought you were. You are not unlike each other."

Charles drew himself up rather stiffly, glanced at his signet ring, whereon the arms of the Hauberk family were engraved, and proceeded to the door.

"No, stay, Charles," said Herbert. "You have heard the beginning of the story, and you may as well hear the end."

"I am not very much interested," said Charles, sitting down, indifferently.

"Well, gentlemen, I have not much to tell. I only saw Bartholomew, if indeed he and Dr. Toogood be the same person," began John—

"Never!" said Mildred.

He then told them that, being left in a state of utter poverty with his sister at X—, he had received a sudden visit from a man whom he described, and whose description tallied exactly with Herbert's conception of Bartholomew, who had inquired into their case, and who came the next day, bringing them the wherewithal to travel to San Francisco, where their mother lived. He added the details about the bag and the umbrella, and finished his short story by saying that he trusted to God that this man, whom they had always cherished in their hearts as their benefactor, for whom they had so often prayed together, might not turn out to be the same villain that Herbert was seeking.

"Of that, I am afraid, there is no doubt," said Herbert.

"What could have been his meaning in giving you the bag and umbrella?" asked Charles.

"He sent it," said Mildred, "as a present to some unknown person. He told us so. You remember, John. He was too good to lie."

"That was only to put the X— people off the scent," said Herbert. "It was even more atrociously arranged than we imagined."

"I am afraid," said John, going up to Mildred

and throwing his arm round her neck, "I am afraid, Mildred dear, that Dr. Toogood was a bad man. He only used us. It was no kindness, but villainy. Do you remember what you told me after you had kissed him?"

"Yes," said Mildred, mournfully.

"We must forget him, dear," said John.

"No, John. He did us a kind act, whatever his motive was. We must not forget that. We are obliged to him."

"No longer by the ties of gratitude. Our obligation is one of money. We must try and find out his whereabouts, and repay him what he has lent us."

A long conversation ensued, discussing the affair. John fully forgave Herbert when he had heard the details, and found the mistake so amusing, that he kept going off into fits of laughter, in which, after a time, Herbert was fain to join. Charles was rather sulky. The idea of confounding a Hauberk with a Dixon-Lovell! Mildred seemed sad. She was combating with the truth. She did not like to think of the Doctor as a bad man.

As the evening drew on they got quite sociable over a bottle of Lacrimæ Christi wine, which John Merton ordered in. They had plenty to talk about. Both Charles and Herbert found the young man and his sister as kind and generous as they were intelligent.

Herbert arranged to stay at the pension for a few days. He said he had not the courage to go back again, and wanted to get his mind settled again. A room was assigned to him near Charles.

That night, as he was getting into bed, Charles knocked, came in, and going up to Herbert, took his hand, saying, "I was offended at being mistaken for your brother. I have come to say that I wish I had a brother like you; I wish I were half so worthy, so good, so true, even so much a gentleman, as you."

"I am only a brewer's adopted son," said Herbert, with a warm grasp of his friend's hand, "and you—well, I know what blood you have in you. I wish, too, my dear fellow, that I had a brother like you. Let us be very good friends. There was no offence. I saw what you felt. I would have explained at the time, only my head was too full of Bartholomew. What a nice girl that Mildred is. Do you know—I think I shall stay on here."

CHAPTER III.

WHAT BECAME OF ESTHER.

Copy of letter from Miss Sabine Crosthwaite, *fianceé* Hiram, to Miss Dorothy Crosthwaite, spinster, of Laburnum Cottage, Keswick.

"Grosvenor Gardens,
"London, W.

"My Dear Dorothy,

"I have been talking to Bartlemy about your unkind behaviour, and the way in which he has urged me to forgive you, proves more than anything else what a sweet disposition is his! He says that bliss being mine I ought to distil sweetness around me, and I quite agree with him. You have been very nasty and unsisterlike to me, but I can, and will, forget it. I am about to become the bride of a good and holy man, and far be it from me to bring rancour between him and his new relations. You know, or perhaps as you live at Keswick you don't know, that in the drama it is a rule that the three affinities should be preserved. I don't know what the three affinities are, but certainly a sister is one, and therefore applying this rule to social life, I wish to preserve you as a sister, and not as a spiteful enemy. I know it must 'rile' (this is Barty's expression) you to see me married while you remain single, but it can't be helped. Women race to the altar, as Dickens says. We must take our chance.

"I write, therefore, to ask you to our wedding, which is definitely fixed for Monday three weeks. It will be quiet and inexpensive. It is a particular good trait in my bridegroom's character that he desires me to spend as little money as possible on myself.

"I have had a full settlement of my money made on myself, capital and interest, so that poor Bartie can't touch one penny without my consent. He opposed this very much, asking if I had no confidence in him; but he gave in in the end, and everything is comfortably settled.

"Our plans for our wedded life are not quite settled yet. We think of going a trip to Normandy or Paris, or perhaps to Guernsey for two or three weeks. Bartie has determined to give up his cure of souls at St. Olphage's, and rest awhile before taking another appointment. We shall perhaps settle in London after our honeymoon, or else find a place in the country.

"We are to be married by special licence, for Bartie is so modest and retiring that he does not want his name published abroad, at the Mary Magdalen Chapel, in Dupeher Street, W., and we shall leave London that same night.

"Now, with reference to another matter. You remember when you were in London last, when you made yourself so disagreeable to me that I had to refuse to see you, you had an adventure —not a creditable one, let me say—with a young woman whom you picked up in the street. It appears that you kept her two days in Grosvenor Hotel, and had doctors and lawyers to consult with her, as if she was anything but what is too disgraceful to mention. You were called away to Keswick suddenly on the same day, and had no time to hear the whole story which the young person had to tell you. You were always very silly, and you have exceeded your silliness here. You sent the lawyer to me to arrange the affair for you. Mr. Bennett came, and began stating the affair, when Bartlemy, who was in the room, jumped up and said—

"'Sir, this is not fit for ladies' ears.'

"The lawyer stopped and said he had been charged by Miss Crosthwaite to tell it to me. Bartlemy said—

"'This lady is soon to be my wife, anything that interests her interests me, and she, having full confidence in me, will allow me to arrange the matter. Sabine leave the room, this is not fit for you to hear.'

"I went. I love obeying so dear and good a man, and left them alone. I don't know what he did, or what was arranged. Bartlemy said it was a case for charity, and that he was grateful to me for bringing it under his notice. He asked me for £50 to settle the affair, which I gave him. I shall be glad to have the £50 back from you, as, you know, I cannot do your charities and mine also.

"I don't know why you have not written to me

all this month, but I forgive you that with other offences.

"Your affectionate sister,

"SABINE."

"P.S.—When you come up to London you had better put up at the Grosvenor again, as I am afraid I shall not have much room in my house for you."

"P.P.S.—Don't forget the £50."

Dorothy was vexed with this letter. It came at the same time as Charles' letter from the Villa Castiglione. Sabine's hurt her less than Charles'. She loved Charles almost better than her sister. The two coming together were very hard. Her state of mind, when she received these letters has been already described.

This is the place to relate as accurately as possible what had taken place between Dorothy, Esther, and John Bennett on the second day of their being together, which, partly owing to the slackness of the post-office officials and partly to Charles' carelessness in losing Dorothy's second letter, has been withheld from the reader's knowledge for some time.

It will be remembered that as soon as Miss Crosthwaite introduced the woman to Lawyer Bennett, Lawyer Bennett had appeared to recognise her. We have had the story as far as where he broke out with the cry of "If only Lord Brookshire!" for such was his exclamation.

Let Dorothy, who is truthful enough, in all sooth, finish the story in the words she often used when talking about the sequel of her adventure.

"No sooner had Lawyer Bennett mentioned his lordship's name, than the young woman, giving a cry of shame, fell fainting at my feet. I looked at him for a moment. Down he went on his knees and took her head into his arms.

"'What a clumsy fellow I am,' he said. 'There, there, dear. Don't take on so.'

"My indefatigable little chambermaid and I soon came to the rescue; of course women know more about these things than law-book men, but it took a good deal of time to get her restored, and when she did, she looked so wretched, so ill, so scared, that I told the lawyer that he must not make any more talk.

"He answered, most politely and kindly, 'I am very sorry for the poor girl's faintness ; but do you know, madam, that I have been looking for this lady for years, at least if I am not mistaken as to her identity, which, after what has occurred, is not probable. However, I see no chance at present of indulging in a lawyer's favourite recreation, cross-examining, and I will come again in two hours. This will really be the best business I have done for years, besides doing several people an inestimable service.'

"With this he departed, leaving me in great astonishment. I could not understand him at all. How could this poor girl be connected with a member of the House of Lords? How did all these strange meetings come about? What a worry and a flurry I was in! Really poor little Dorothy's head had begun to turn.

"The woman was better in a few minutes. She began to speak. She kept repeating—

"'Is he gone? Oh, don't let him see me! No, no, don't let him see me! He will do me a mischief; he will, he will indeed.'

"I said—'My dear girl, I think Mr. Bennett is the last person who would do anybody any injury.'

"'Yes he will. Oh, don't let me see him! Tell me that he is gone. I cannot see him. I shall go mad. Everything is so horrible. Oh, do not let me see him!'

"I said, 'Well, my dear, if you do not want to see him I don't see why you should. You are under my protection, a weak little woman's protection it is true, but the weak little woman is sturdy, and you shan't be touched.'

"She was too weak to reply, but took my hand and kissed it gratefully.

"I continued, 'But he is coming back in two hours.'

"'No, no,' cried she in a weak voice. 'No, no, I can't see him,' and so saying she rose to her feet and staggered across the room towards the door.

"'Stay,' said I, gently detaining her, 'you must not go like that; you must talk to me first. Are you really frightened of this good man?'

"'Yes, yes, yes!' cried she, rising again.

"'Well,' said I, 'if that's the case, I do not

see why you should see him. I'll take you away at once.'

"'Please, please,' said she, sinking on her knees. 'Dear lady, take me away any—anywhere. Take me back to the street where you found me. Let me die in the gutter, but do not let any more shame come upon me.'

"I did not know what to do. I felt so perplexed that I thought of running away. You see Dorothy is not always sensible. I did, I really did think of running back all the way to Keswick. Was not a sensible idea? But I didn't. I began to think more rationally, and then I said—

"'You shan't be put to any more suffering, child. You shall come away. He is coming back in two or three hours, and then you must be gone. As soon as we are ready we will go.'

"Her only answer was another kiss on Dorothy's wrinkled hand. I ordered some tea, and we were both glad of the refreshment. I let her rest awhile. It was not much good, for at every footfall she started, her black eyes rolling wildly, and cried, 'Oh, there he is! Oh, let us go!'

"In about an hour I ordered a cab, and giving her a cloak to throw over her head went downstairs with her on my arm. The waiters stared rather, and one or two pert maids giggled. I got her out into the cab. Then, of course, the driver asked, 'Where to, madam?' I declare I did not know. I thought of saying, 'To Laburnum Cottage,' but that was absurd. I looked first at the cabman and then at the woman, who had sunk back into a corner. At last remembering the name I said, 'Charing Cross.'

"As we were driving there I began to think. Here was a nice state of affairs for a simple country woman. No more London adventures for me, thank you. At last I hit on a plan. Oh, wasn't I thankful when I had thought it out. I took out my purse. I had cashed a cheque for fifty pounds that morning, and had the money in my pocket still.

"I did not speak to the poor lady; I had addressed her once or twice, but she could not answer. She kept repeating, 'Take me away, take me away;' and that was all she ever said.

"Well, my plan was arranged. It was the best I could think of. When we got to Charing Cross the driver stopped, and asked if we were for the station.

"'No,' said I, 'go to the first saddlery shop you see.'

"He obeyed, and I got out at a shop in the Strand, where they sold portmanteaus. I bought a little leather one, and directed the driver to a dress shop. Here I bought sundry things for the woman, two new gowns, some blue ribbon for her hair, for I thought how much better she would look with her hair nicely smoothed down and tied up behind with a little blue ribbon, some under-clothing, in fact, a complete outfit.

"I then said to the driver—

"'Where can I get cheap lodgings?'

"He looked at me and whistled.

"'So you're a boltin', are you?' said he.

"I told him that I did not understand him, but would he kindly drive me where I asked. He said there were comfortable lodgings at the Queen's Hotel, Newgate, or at the Stone Jug Inn, Pentonville. I said I did not want to go to either an hotel or an inn. He laughed. I do not know what I should have done had not a commissionaire come by at that moment; a nice civil man. He asked me if he could serve me. I said yes. I asked him to find me a cheap lodging, not in the centre of the city. He said he was at my service, and asked me where I should like to go to. I said it was immaterial, as long as it was in a quiet, airy street. He said his missus, his wife I presumed, had a lodging to let in Burton Row, Westminster. Would that suit? I said we would see. He then got on to the box and we drove through Westminster, by the side of the Thames, and up a little street. We stopped before a little clean-looking house in a row of houses. He got down and let us in. His wife was a very nice motherly person. I said I wanted lodging for a lady. Had she one? She showed me a clean, tidy little room on the upper floor, neatly furnished and altogether comfortable-looking. I was then forced to tell a story. I said the lady was a poor relation of mine, who had been ill and had been ordered change of air. I asked her if she would undertake to board and lodge her, and do her washing. The woman assented. I then asked her her terms. She said she would take her for 35s. per week, all included.

I said that would suit. I asked her for a receipt for eight weeks in advance. She wrote it and I paid her fifteen pounds. The extra sovereign, I said, was to see that she took good care of her lodger. The woman thanked me, and said it was not necessary. She would do her best. I begged her to keep it. I then conducted Esther up stairs, and the husband carried up the trunk. I asked the woman to light a fire and prepare the room, and also to get some tea ready. While she was doing this, I spoke seriously to the lady. I said I would leave her there, apparently in good hands, and I hoped she would soon get well, and hear from her friends. I told her I would write to her from home, and would see that I kept her whereabouts secret. I then gave her the receipt and ten pounds in cash. She took them, but they dropped from her hands. She did not speak. I put the money into her pocket and took the receipt away with me. I then committed her to the woman's care, and told her to look well after her. Mrs. Martin, for such was the woman's name, said she would. I then bent over the poor lady and kissed her. She kissed me back, but said nothing.'

"I said, 'My dear girl, I must go now. I think you will be comfortable here, and at any rate you must stay till you hear from your friends. Your rent and board are paid for two months, and you have enough to go on with. I do not think you have done anything wrong. I am sure not. I wish I could come and see you again, but that, I fear, is impossible. I return home to-night. Will you tell me your name?'

"'Esther,' she answered.

"'Esther what?'

"'Esther, Esther, Esther.'

"'Well, then, Esther be it,' said I. 'I will write to you, and you will write to me. If you like to tell me anything I shall be very pleased, but don't if you don't care to, and don't think me anything too kind. My dear, dear girl, I wish I could help all my poor sisters and brothers. But that is, of course, impossible.'

"I then explained that I really must be gone, but she looked so ill that I could not go till, with the aid of kind Mrs. Martin, I had put her to bed, and tucked her up warmly before the cheerful fire. I then kissed her again, and all she said was 'thank you,' but at the same time she pointed to the sky. I understood her, and I do hope that He is not displeased with me. I had thought of Him all the time, and the thought of His sacrifice, so great, so complete, had quelled any little selfish remonstrances I had made to myself.

"Once more commending her to Mrs. Martin's charge, I entered the cab. I offered the man something for his trouble but he refused. The cabman was very surly, and drove so slowly that it was quite seven before we got home.

"I found poor Mr. Bennett waiting patiently for me, in the hotel secretary's office. He at once asked me how Esther was. I said she had gone.

"'Gone?' said he, 'gone?'

"'Yes, gone,' said I.

"I could not explain all to him. I did not want to let him know her whereabouts, for she had appeared frightened of him, and though he looked a good man, I did not know whether I ought to break her confidence.

"I told him that she had asked me to let her go, and that she had gone. He asked me if I knew where she had gone to. I said I could not tell.

"He said, rather impatiently, 'But I must know.'

"I was firm, and he was pressing.

"He said, 'It is most important. My business is most important.'

"I answered, 'Yes, sir, but my promise is more important.'

"He did not press me much more, but he seemed very vexed. I was sorry, as he was a kind man, but then I had promised to say nothing, and I had told enough stories already.

"At last, when he found out he could get no information from me, he rose, saying—

"'I am very sorry, madam, that you have so little confidence in me. I assure you I would rather have paid five thousand pounds than have lost sight of that lady.'

"I said, 'She is in good hands.'

"He said, 'I know, I know that you have done your best, but if you knew the interests at stake, even her interests, you would not refuse me what I ask.'

"I said I could not tell him.

"He then asked me if I would hear the story and its connection with Esther, and though I was rather curious I felt so utterly tired and shaken that I told him I would rather wait. Then, remembering I had to go to Keswick next morning to be present at the wedding of one of our old servant's daughters, which I had promised to attend, I told him my sister's address, and asked him to be so kind as to give her the details, which she would then communicate to me.

"He agreed, but as he went he said, 'I believe you, madam, to be kind and just. You are now doing an unkindness and an injustice, though you do not mean it. For the last time. Honour, riches, and the good name of many, even of her, are at stake. Will you answer me—where is she?'

"Was it obstinacy, or what? I answered, 'I cannot.'

"He departed, refusing any money for his trouble. He seemed very downcast.

"Next day I went to Keswick. In three days I wrote to Esther, at Mrs. T. Martin's, 18, Burton's Row, Westminster. I had a line in answer from Mrs. Martin, saying that Mrs. Esther was getting on nicely, and sent me her love. I wrote to Sabine two or three times, but my letters were returned through the post, in envelopes addressed in a strange hand, which I since found out to be that of the *bridegroom*.

At the end of eight weeks Dorothy had again

written to Mrs. Martin about Esther, and learned from her that she had been visited by a tall gentleman during the last week. One of Mrs. Martin's letters may be of interest. Here is a copy of it:—

"18, Burton's Row,
"Westminster, London.

"MADAM,

"I write in answer of yours kindly, of yesterday asking for information about the lady, Mrs. Esther, as you left in my charge, kindly paying five-teen pounds for her lodging, board, firing, and washing therein inclooded. She has been much better lately, and very cheerful in her little ways, never complaining, and being quite the lady in all things. She got quite strong after a bit, and used to take walks into the town. Two days ago she came in, flurried-like and ran upstairs. Shortly afterwards their came a tall gentleman, who nocks and asts as if Mrs. Ester were at home. I asted his name. He said it were John Benet, I showed him up and left him. Suddenly he came running down the stair, quicker nor when he went up. He came agin yesterday, and went up the stair on his toes, and walked in to er room. I had a job for to do in the next room, hers adjoining, and could not elp earing their talk.

"Says he, 'I know yer now, I know yer sister's game.' She says nothing.

"On goes he with, 'So don't talk no more of revinge on me, but keep quiet, if you would have me do likewise, for I can talk, knowing all.'

"She must have upped and at him, for I heerd him tumblin about the room, and what the furnitoor would suffer, little could I know. Then he came running out the room, and I pops my head on to the landing, and says, sneering like—

"'Look ere, Master Benet, don't you come ere no more.'

"But he were off before them words of mine ad taken effect.

"To-day, being the end of the eight weeks, she packs her trunk, and says she must go. She has just gone in a 'ansome,' and a grey orse, and a driver who does not know where to stop in his liquer, as wanted to kiss my Mary Jane, coming ome with the milk, which shows his imperence more nor words of mine can tell.

"I'm sorry she's gone, I liked her. She gave no address, but told me to thank you again and again. She have a solemn way with her sometimes.

"Not remembering more to say, and John having come home, as wants his tea,

"I remain, with respecks,

"Yours obediently,

"REBECCA MARTIN."

When Dorothy received this letter, she at once sent a copy of it to her sister, but added the full account of her interview with Esther, not sparing Hiram, and yet not doing him any injustice. This letter was returned in the same way as the others. She endeavoured to get the letter re-transmitted to Sabine by a circuitous route, by sending it through a friend, but it came back as before. During the latter end of March she was away, and did not return to Keswick till the beginning of April, when she wrote again. The same result. At last she gave up writing, with a sad heart. It was towards the end of April that she received the letter from Sabine, a copy of which is given above. She determined to be present at the wedding, to do her best to make it pass off pleasantly for her sister. She pitied her, but seeing that her fate was inevitable, she determined not to embitter, what she clearly foresaw would be an unhappy marriage, by unpleasantness on her part, and resolved, now that Hiram was to become her relation, to endeavour to find out the good in him, and to close her eyes to the past, and now that Esther was lost sight of, to forget the whole story. She wrote to Sabine—

"Dear Sister,

"I will be at your wedding. May you be very, very happy, and, though married, still keep a little space in your heart for your truly affectionate and loving sister.

"Dorothy."

Charles's letter she put aside. It was blotted with tears.

True to her resolution not to revert to a memory which could only serve to awaken her indignation at her sister's future husband, she made no allusion to it in her subsequent letters to Charles. It is true, at the time, she had told him all, but she did not again refer to it.

It has already been explained how Charles did not get to know the story. Might it have interested him? Might it?

CHAPTER IV.

WEDDING BELLS.

At about the same time that Herbert arrived at Sorrento, in search of Milwaukee Bartholomew, that gentleman was celebrating his nuptials, under the name and designation of the Rev. Bartlemy Hiram, with Miss Sabine Crosthwaite.

The eventful morning having arrived, the good people of 3, Grosvenor Gardens, W., were in no small state of excitement. Sabine had nearly lost her head, and was divided between the distraction of giving the final touches to the breakfast table, and the excitement of putting on her bridal robes. The sun shone cheerfully through the drawing-room windows on the company assembled there, preparatory to going to church. There was Mrs. Lipp-Sirva, of garrulous celebrity, Mrs. Tatelry-Taylor, of Keswick, Colonel Stoat, of Winchester, and other ladies and gentlemen. Of Dorothy's friends there were few; neither Mr. Hirdon, the trustee, nor Mr. Hardwick, the family solicitor, were present. They had excused themselves on the plea of business. In truth, they were both too manly to assist at so ludicrous a wedding.

Dorothy was there in a simple gown, maroon in colour, which gave offence to Sabine. Said Sabine—

"The idea of putting on maroon at a wedding! Are not white lace and orange flowers cheap enough?"

"They are cheap enough," answered Dorothy. "But white lace don't go with grey hairs, and orange flowers do not suit spectacles."

Sabine huffed and said nothing. It was obvious that Dorothy was determined to spoil her wedding. Indeed during the whole service Sabine thought more of Dorothy's inharmonious dress than of the solemn words of the minister.

Of Dorothy's personal friends there were only two, a Colonel Markham, a brother-in-arms of her father, and the Rev. John Troutbeck, a cousin, who had been invited by Sabine on the express condition that Dorothy should contribute to the expense of the breakfast.

The marriage was to take place at eleven, the bridegroom to be in attendance at the church, the St. Mary Magdalen Chapel, in Dupeher Street.

Dorothy did her best to be of use to her sister in this trying event. Sabine went about in a fixed, obstinate, set-teeth way, and was very excited, and did not receive her sister's attentions with much amiability.

The conversation in the drawing-room was not very lively. Sabine's friends appeared not to mix readily with Dorothy's. Colonel Markham, a tired old soldier, who had fought through the Indian Mutiny, looked as if he was present at the execution of an unhappy Sepoy. The Rev. John Troutbeck kept feeding Sabine's canaries, till those wretched birds must have fancied themselves being fattened for the table. Mrs. Lipp-Sirva and Mrs. Tatelry-Taylor were exchanging congratulations on this most happy occasion. The other ladies were indulging in the usual vapid drawing-room talk, while a young man, whose claim to be at the wedding nobody clearly understood, was composing on the back of a millinery bill of Sabine's, a set of verses on Hymen, in which the words—

> Said the sprightly young lover to the queenly Sabine,
> Oh! marry me, darling, and then you'll be mine.

occurred as the refrain.

At last it was time to be off. The carriages came round, and the people drove off to Dupeher Street. The Rev. John Troutbeck, with Colonel Markham, Mrs. Lipp-Sirva, and Mrs. Tatelry-Taylor, and the other ladies in different carriages. Sabine was accompanied by Dorothy and Colonel Stoat. The young man, who had been busy with the eighteenth and last verse of his poem, did not manage to secure a seat in any of the carriages. The unfinished poem was afterwards found pasted with a wafer to the drawing-room-door; the young man was not seen again.

During the drive, which was a long one, Dorothy put a prayer-book into Sabine's hand, turning down the leaf of a page. It had grieved her to see Sabine without any book, and that in the midst of all her preparations she had not shown that she considered the religious part of the ceremony in the least. The action was well meant, but Colonel Stoat found it ridiculous, and laughed. Sabine flushed up and tossed the book on to the botton of the carriage, with a "Don't bother, Dorothy."

Dorothy picked the book up. It was a beautifully bound little book, which she had bought for a wedding present for her sister. On the fly-leaf she had written—

To Sabine Hiram, from her loving sister.

It hurt her, this action of her sister ; it seemed to her a token of the estrangement which was to arise between her sister and herself. She was not well ; her head had burned all the morning, but she had patiently done her best to be cheerful and amiable to her sister. She said nothing, but put her hand up to her forehéad, and bent her head. Were they tears ? Was it a prayer ?

At the chapel they found Mr. Hiram, quite alone. His best man, who was afterwards introduced to the company as C. Snorker, Esquire, had not yet come. The reverend gentleman was dressed in his usual style, and in his black suit, black tie, and black kid gloves, looked more like an attendant at a funeral than a happy bridegroom. His umbrella, which acted a mute Pylades to his Orestes, was leaning in the porch.

When the company arrived, they found the happy man standing in the aisle reading a newspaper, and taking an occasional survey of the empty pews.

The parson and the clerk were heard talking

in the vestry. The clergyman was expressing his wish that this job might soon be over, as he had several funerals to attend to that day.

When Hiram saw his bride and her friends, he stuffed the newspaper into the pocket of his black frock coat, and advanced smiling. Colonel Stoat shook him warmly by the hand, Dorothy bowed, and Sabine tried to giggle. The rest of the company were put into their places in the front seats.

Mr. C. Snorker then appeared; he had been refreshing himself at the Belle-Alliance Inn, round the corner of Dupeher Street. He was dressed in a blue frock-coat, check trousers, patent leather boots, and lavender tie and gloves.

The parson was ready and looked as if he wished the people would make haste. The service was gabbled through hastily. Colonel Stoat gave the bride away. During the service, when Hiram was munificently endowing his bride with all his worldly goods, C. Snorker was heard to suppress a chuckle. Hiram caught Dorothy's eye and quailed.

The vestry business was soon got over, with the usual kisses and congratulations.

Bartlemy entered his name thus:

"(Mi) Bartlemy Hiram—29—Clerk in holy orders. Son of Herbert Hiram, gentleman."

He began to sign his name "Mi," which he quickly erased. C. Snorker was the only witness who noticed it. He nudged Hiram's arm, who immediately rectified his mistake.

As soon as the register was signed, the clergyman assumed his funeral service look. The company returned together to Grosvenor Gardens. Sabine, Dorothy, Bartlemy and C. Snorker, Esq., drove home together. Bartlemy appeared very happy, Sabine in bliss, Dorothy chatting pleasantly, and Snorker in high spirits. Bartlemy kept kissing his bride, and I believe Snorker tried to do the same to her bridesmaid. Dorothy, at heart, felt weary and utterly disgusted, but she hid it well beneath a kindly mask, and did her best to please.

The breakfast was not a great success. The talk was not general. Colonel Markham eyed the bridegroom, who was eating as if he had been starving for days, with evident disfavour. The ladies, pretending to peck at things, ate each enough to nourish a workman's family for twenty-four hours. The speeches were not good. C. Snorker became excited, and talked in an extraordinarily incoherent manner. He made a speech, and in the middle of it, to Dorothy's infinite pain and disgust, fell under the table. This incident gave the cue to break up, and the company rose.

Colonel Markham departed at once with his friend the Rev. John Troutbeck. Some of the ladies went also. Snorker was carried upstairs, singing the not thoroughly appropriate Hymen, Hymenæe of "Waiter, here Pst, Pst."

Only Mrs. Lipp-Sirva and Mrs. Tatelry-Taylor remained; they had not finished their meal. Dorothy helped Sabine to change her dress.

Bartlemy went on refreshing himself at the sideboard. He had been singularly silent all the morning. His scar had never been so prominent; it glowed like a line of dull fire on his sallow cheek. His eyes glittered with an expression of appeased avarice and triumph. Not the slightest vestige of shame appeared to trouble him, no remorse at what he was doing, no trepidation, no fear of exposure seemed to occupy his thoughts. He was happy, as a wild beast is happy. He exulted, he had gained the day. Money and comfort were once more in his grasp, and this was happiness to him. There are on earth and in our midst, men who are living problems; men who appear to personify that terrible principle, perverseness; men who appear to give in their persons denial to the creed that they are the creatures of a Being of Infinite Goodness. They are the hyænas, the sharks, of the class Homo. They are horrible to contemplate, but interesting to study.

It had been arranged that the newly-married couple should take a trip to Paris before settling in London, and they departed for the Continent that day. The house was left in charge of Mrs. Lipp-Sirva. Dorothy went back to Keswick in a state of dreary misery. She had seen a wretched farce played out, a farce without humour, a farce in which her dearly beloved sister acted the dupe to the Scapin of a miserable, common, vulgar man. She had tried to persuade herself that all might go well; she had tried to believe Sabine could be happy, but the whole ceremony, its marked incidents, the coldness of her friends Markham and Troutbeck, in whose good sense she had unbounded confidence, and finally the disgusting behaviour of her brother-in-law's friend, had opened her eyes completely. She could foresee nothing but shame and misery for her sister. Was not that enough to trouble her? And then there was Charles, her dear boy. What was he doing? Why did he not write? Why had he not written lately? Why had he never written to revoke his unkind expressions towards her? Why was all so unhappy?

She kept up well enough till she got home again. She was able to go about her little affairs for a day or two. She tried to fall back into her old life, but the figure of her brother-in-law haunted her. She could not sleep; she had no comfort.

* * * * *

It was Sabine's bridal night. They were staying at Clarendon Hotel, Dover. She was alone in her chamber, preparing for rest. A candle was burning low in its socket, shedding a fitful light about the room; the fire burning low. She heard a step in the passage. Was it the bridegroom?

Suddenly a mighty gust of wind, blown from the embanking sea-mist landwards, blew the casement open with a crash, extinguished the light, and went howling through the long corridors of the hotel. Sabine jumped to her feet with a startled cry. Another cry, louder than the first; for, turning to the opened window, she saw standing there in the light of the cloud-veiled moon, a tall figure pointing seawards. It was the figure of a woman dressed in a black mantle, with a cape drawn over her head. Paralyzed with horror, Sabine moved neither hand nor foot. The figure turned, and the moon, bursting through the black clouds, revealed her face. It was the grinning face of a death's head. Sabine fell, with a shriek that rang through the house, to the ground.

It was thus that the bridegroom found his bride. This was Sabine's bridal night, and never since that night could she be brought to believe that the vision was only engendered by an excited imagination. She believed firmly that she had seen in actual reality a tall dark figure, robed in black, with the grinning face of a death's head mask pointing seawards, in her bridal chamber, on the vesper of her bridal night. Was it an omen? Was it a dream?

CHAPTER V.

THE TWO SISTERS.

Two days after her arrival at Keswick Dorothy received this note from her sister, announcing their safe arrival at Paris :—

"Hotel Continental, Paris.

"My Dear Dorothy,

"We have arrived here safely. Paris is a beautiful town. Bartlemy is a dear pet, and I am quite happy.

"By the bye, could you lend me £50? I have spent all my ready money, and have no more till next quarter day. My husband's tenants in the Scilly Islands, where his property lies, have not paid their rents, and he is wisely unwilling to sell out any of his bank stock, so that he, too, is unprovided with money. I did not know of this before we left London, or I would have arranged against it. I thought he would be sure to be provided with the necessary funds, but I am not angry with him, as he is acting wisely in not selling out, and if his tenants won't pay, they won't.

"Your affectionate sister,

"Sabine Hiram."

Now it so happened that when Dorothy received

this letter she was not only seriously indisposed, but owing to the expenses incidental to her sister's wedding, her journey to London, the hotel bill there, and especially owing to unexpected claims that had been made on her bounty about that time, she was not prepared with £50.

One thousand pounds a year may seem a good sum as an income, but when there are many people pulling at the purse it does not go a long way. Besides, Dorothy was not what one might call a thorough business woman even in her own personal expenses. Not that she was extravagant. Oh, no! she was far too good a steward of her father's bounty to be that, but she had been so long kept without much money of her own that when, after her father's death, she entered upon an independent income, she did not quite understand how to manage it.

She was very sorry to have to refuse Sabine, but she did, as this note will show:—

"Laburnum Cottage, Keswick.

"MY DEAREST SABINE,

"I am so sorry to have to say, that until the L.N.W. dividends come in, I have no money to spare. I have been rather extravagant lately, I am afraid. I have had a good scolding from one or two friends about it. As it is, I cannot send you the £50. Your husband had better sell out for a little ready money, and when his rents come in he can re-invest. I am so glad to hear you are happy in your new estate, and most sincerely hope you will continue so.

"I myself have not been at all well lately; bad headaches and giddiness. Doctor says I ought to go out more, but I get very tired when I do.

"I hope to hear from you soon, that you may have got over your difficulty, and are still enjoying your trip.

"Give my compliments to your husband, and with much love to yourself, believe me, dear Sabine, your very affectionate sister,

"DOROTHY CROSTHWAITE."

(When Dorothy wrote this letter she had just £7 in her pocket, two of which were promised to a poor old woman at Bowness, whose son had been drowned in Lake Windermere in a boating accident.)

Sabine wrote back by return of post:—

"Hotel Continental, Paris.

"*Miss* DOROTHY,

"I don't think you are acting either kindly or sisterly to me to refuse me the money. When you were helping a London slut I lent you £50, and you might do the same. However, I shan't ask you again, and as my time is fully taken up with my husband you had better stop writing. I am sorry you are ill. You have brought it on yourself by carelessness.

"*Mrs.* SABINE HIRAM."

This was the finishing stroke. Dorothy was sitting in her cheerful little parlour when she received this letter. She had felt better all day. There had been bright sunshine all the morning, and she had taken a little walk by the lake-side. The cheering effects of the exercise and of the warm sunshine had warmed her heart a little and done her spirits and body good, and she felt more like her old self again when she came in. That day happened to be the anniversary of the General's death, and was quite a holyday to Dorothy. It was this day, that she devoted her thoughts especially to the sturdy old father who had brought her up strongly and steadfastly. On this day it was her wont to read his letters, laying before her on the table a lock of grey hair which she cut from the dear head when its eyes had closed that sad afternoon so few years ago for an eternal sleep. By the side of the grey hair she laid her father's sword, propping a portrait of him against the butt, and by its side his gold watch. Thus, with all the relics of the dear dead about her, she communed with her thoughts, remembering all the happy times she had had at home with her manly old father, dwelling with affection on the remembrance of the many times when, for all his apparent severity, he had stooped to caress "his little woman" and forgetting all his harshness.

The thought of her father and of her happy home naturally brought Dorothy's thoughts to her sister, and to the dear brothers lying far from each other in foreign graves, and the pleasant times, now so long ago, they had had together. Then she began to laugh at herself for having harboured any triste presentiments, and was persuading herself that all would go well, and that Sabine in her happiness would forget old grievances and be a dear sister to her once more, when the letter came. Dorothy read it. It was too much. Sadly she gathered up the relics of her father, laid them in their places, and then she went to bed. Dorothy was very ill.

CHAPTER VI.

WHAT A WORLD OF HAPPINESS THEIR HARMONY FORETELLS!

It did not take very long to open Sabine's eyes to the real character and position of her husband.

Mr. Hiram acted the part of the impassioned lover with tolerable accuracy, though every now and then he would burst out laughing in the midst of some touching scene, as if he were acting in a farce and was so amused that he could not contain himself.

It was only during the second week of their honeymoon, that the first storm broke out. They were sitting at breakfast in their sitting-room in the Hôtel Continental, discussing their plans for the day's amusement. This naturally brought them on to the topic of the expenses thereof, and it was then that Sabine remarked—

"Bartie, dear, when will you receive your remittances? You know we want money, and mine has quite run out, and now that nasty Dorothy won't lend me any, I have none to go on with till next quarter day."

Bartlemy said, "You must sell out, dear; you must sell out. Money must be had."

"But can't you do so?" said Sabine. "You know you can re-invest when your rents come in."

Bartlemy burst into a loud guffaw and nearly

choked himself with his coffee. When he had recovered he said—

"No-o, Sabine, I cannot."

"Why not?"

"Because"—

"Because what?"

"Because rum-diddle-diddle-dee fol-lol-la."

"Neither rum-diddle-diddle-dee nor fol-lol-la will supply us with means to pay our bill here, or to take us our carriage drives.

Bartlemy said nothing, but lit a Manilla.

Sabine was vexed at his treating the matter so lightly, so she said rather snappishly—

"I don't think that is the way to treat me, and I don't think you ought to smoke those nasty cigars in my room."

"These are not cigars, my pet."

"What then?"

"Manillas, my cherub of cherubim."

"Well, Manillas, then. I won't have such ways in my room."

"*Your* room, Sabine, your room?"

"Yes, *my* room, *my* room."

"My room, dearest, the husband's room, what is mine is thine, and thine, angel, is mine, don't yer know?"

But Sabine was thoroughly vexed. She began to fear that Hiram had only married her for her money, and that he had nothing of his own. Ever since his wedding day (to buy the ring, for which occasion he had borrowed £10 of her), he had never ceased to plague her for money. Often, too, he had gone out, leaving her alone all the evening, to return late at night. Now Sabine was both avaricious and exacting, and therefore Hiram was just acting in the very way to get into her black books.

He did not seem to care, though, for, sitting in true American style, with his chair tilted up and his feet on the marble mantel-piece, he continued to smoke quietly, blowing huge clouds of smoke between himself and his wife.

Now be it that the pungent vapour of the Manilla irritated Sabine's mucous membrane, or be it that some wandering fly, sent by a god inimical to Hymen, alighted on that lady's nose to study the art of engraving on copper, but certain it is that Sabine sneezed once, twice, and both times violently. The violent motion of her head in the process of sternutation, dislodged the row of false curls, arranged as what is commonly called a front, and these fell on her lap. There was not much more wanted to complete her irritation, but Bartlemy laughed, that was more than enough. Sabine rose to her feet in a state of incomprehensible anger, and holding the false curls in her hand, stamped her foot violently on the floor, and burst into a torrent of spiteful reproach.

"You horrid, vulgar man! What have you got to laugh at? Your own wedded wife, too! With your legs on the mantel-piece at the Hôtel Continental—aren't you ashamed of yourself? And what if I do wear false curls? I paid for them, I suppose? When is your money coming? Anything is better than red hair—mine is tightly tied up, and not *one* penny shall you have to spend on sherry-cobblers. Manillas, too, in my drawing-room—you suck through a straw, faugh! And nicely your friend Snorker behaved, too, at the wedding. Staying out all last night—drunk as a lord—and you a clergyman of the Church of England. Why didn't I listen to my friends. What is to become of us if we begin quarrelling now? Oh! I am so disgusted—I'll go home—I won't stay here, to have you smoke in my room. Your tenants, too—disrespectful men they are. When I write to your farmer, Mr. Sharp, to the address you gave in the Scilly Islands, to ask for your rents, what does he do? He insults your wife, your lawful wedded wife; and sends back my letter with 'not known' written on the envelope; and you sit there, with your legs on the mantel-piece."

With these, and many similar reproaches and peevish threats, did Sabine revile her lord and master, but finding that she only seemed to amuse him, she rushed out of the room, banging the door violently after her.

Hiram looked round, and spitting a quantity of tobacco juice after her as she closed the door, got up.

"Whew!" said he, "Is this the way she is going to go on? This won't do. If I have run all this risk, and had all this bother, and faked my cards, to turn up a black deuce in the end, I'm a bigger fool than I thought I was. Esther was better than she. Esther, at least, was young and pretty; but that old cow! If she had not got her money tied up she'd be a dear bargain, but as it is, deuced if I don't think I'm sold. Still, a thousand a year certain, five thousand dollars, are comfortable enough. But I haven't patience. I shall lob her by-and-bye, if she goes on this suit, and then all will be U P. I must act otherwise. And, beware Mrs. Hiram the Third, lest you get into an evil plight. I am not the man to scruple or hesitate—but where is that letter from Snorker?"

Bartlemy got up, and after rummaging in his writing-case found a letter addressed to the Rev. Bartlemy Hiram. He opened it and re-read it. It was short and enigmatical.

"DEAR MIL.

"If cash tight, or old girl capricious.

"Peckham Lodge. Twig?

"C. S."

"I hope it may not come to that," said Bartlemy, as he put the letter back into its envelope. "I hardly like that job. Curse Snorker; am I not bad enough without his devilish suggestions? No, no, it must not come to that. I've played a successful game so far, but after the Lord Mayor's show comes the dung cart, and trumps may fail. I must go on as I have done, and try to get what I want. If she is still skittish, well—then will be time to think of Peckham Lodge. And now for my little Palais Royal girl."

That evening, after dinner, Sabine made friends

again with her husband, and gave him some money. He immediately took his hat, and was going to leave the room, when she asked him to stay; she had something so nice to tell him.

"What is it?" said Bartlemy, impatiently. "I want to be off."

"Where to?"

"To the Young Men's Christian Association."

There was a notorious *café* on the boulevards, which Bartlemy frequented at nights, which he pleasantly styled the Young Men's Christian Association, whenever his wife asked him where he had been.

"No, stay," said Sabine, "a gentleman is coming to see you."

"Who is he? What does he want?"

"He is the Rev. John Middleton, chaplain of the English chapel, in the Rue des Capucines. I met him at *table d'hôte.* He is called away to England suddenly for a week and has to provide for the services in his absence. I told him that my husband was a clergyman of the Church of England, and I said I thought you would only be too glad to oblige him."

"You did, did you?" growled Bartlemy.

"Yes, dear, you remember complaining, only yesterday, that you had no work to do, no lambs to attend to. Don't you remember? It was just before you borrowed that fifty francs of me. So when I heard him talking about this difficulty, I at once thought what a nice thing for you."

"And you say that this fellow is coming to-day?"

"Yes, dear, directly."

Bartlemy appeared very much at a loss what to do, or what to say. He stood in the middle of the room, twisting his broad wide-awake hat, and casting ferocious glances at his wife. He had never appeared more repulsively ugly than then.

"I won't see him," he said at last. "I won't be taken in again. If it is known that there is a soft clergyman here in Paris, I shall have every lazy chaplain who wants to get off work running after me to take his duty. Clergymen are not so very zealous when they can get others to do their work. I certainly won't give in this time. Now, listen, Sabine. I don't want you to advertise me at every corner. I don't want to be talked about, and referred about; I am not strong, and I cannot overwork myself. I don't want to do this work. I should not be doing a kindness to the man if I did undertake it. I should only be encouraging him in sloth, and sloth is a bad quality in a clergyman. We all have our work, and we must do it—I at St. Olphage's, Wykeham-Within, and he, at his chapel, in the Rue des Capucines. I suppose he would offer to pay me. I do not make the golden key the bar, but I feel strongly that the hireling fleeth, and that the good shepherd ought to know his sheep, and not leave them to go to England for a week. You may refer him on this subject to the Axe of the Apostles, or St.

Jacob's gospel. I do not know where the passage occurs at this moment. It is in one of those two."

Bartlemy was then going to take his departure, when a knock at the door announced that the Rev. John Middleton had come.

This gentleman, introducing himself with much suavity, asked if he had the pleasure of addressing the Rev. Hiram.

"You have," said Bartlemy, abruptly preparing to leave the room.

The Rev. John Middleton, to judge from his appearance, was one of those sleek self-satisfied parsons who fancy that the fact of their being under the wing of the Church elevates them above the rest of men, and frees them to a certain degree from the conventionalities and etiquette of society. This gentleman carried a "Clergy List" in his hand. He had it open at the letter H. Turning to Sabine he said—

"My dear madam, I have come to apologise. I see that your husband's name does not"—

"Whoever gave you leave to enter my room?" burst out Bartlemy.

"I am addressing your wife, sir," said the Rev. Middleton, with a touch of mild reproach. "I am addressing"—

"I don't want you to address anybody."

"Your dear wife, who kindly suggested that you would undertake to perform my duty during my absence to England."

"My dear wife had not the slightest right to promise anything of the kind."

"Oh! Bartie," said Sabine.

"Oh Bartie, or Bartie Oh! I won't do anything of the kind. I won't encourage absentees. I will not be the hireling of any faithless shepherd, who wishes to go to England for a week."

"I do not now wish it," said Mr. Middleton. "I have come to tell the lady that I have found a substitute. I should have been very much obliged to you, had you acted for me, but as my chapel is strictly Church of England, and as your name does not"—

Bartlemy rushed out of the room.

"Appear in the 'Clergy List,'" continued Mr. Middleton, blandly, "I had to look for another."

"Not appear in the 'Clergy List?'" was the astonished question of Sabine. "What do you mean?"

The Rev. Middleton answered by placing the book in her hands.

True, the name of Hiram appeared nowhere, and turning to the part where the livings are alphabetically arranged, and looking under Wykeham-Within Sabine found the following entry:—

"Wykeham-Within, Kent: Rev. John Marsden, M.A., vicar; Rev. Upland Stylites, curate."

"Is your husband not of our persuasion?" asked Mr. Middleton.

"Yes, yes," said Sabine hurriedly. "Yes; there is some mistake. He is curate of St. Olphage's at Wykeham-Within, or at least was two months ago."

"No, no, madam," said the Rev. John Middleton; "an error, an error. I am the incumbent of the adjoining parish of Wykeham-in-the-Bath, and I know both the Rev. Marsden and the Rev. U. Stylites."

"How long?" asked Sabine faintly.

"Several years; yes, I may say several years."

"Are there not perhaps two curates?" put in Sabine in desperation.

"Madam, not much of glebe, of corn and oil is enjoyed by the vicar. This parish is poor, very poor, and can hardly maintain one minister, let alone three."

"Is there no other church near? no chapel? I am positive that there is Bartlemy's cure."

"I have not heard of any ecclesiastical institution in the parish of Wykeham-Within rejoicing in the denomination of Bartlemy's cure," answered Mr. Middleton. "There is a chapel there not officiated over by either of the gentlemen I have named."

"What is it?"

"A very noisesome nest of Dissent. A kind of American Shakers, or something equally awfully awful."

"Who is the presiding minister?"

"I do not know his name. I have never seen him. Where ignorance is bliss, you know."

"Thank you, sir."

"Pas de quoi, madame."

With this Mr. Middleton departed, leaving Sabine in no very comfortable state of mind. Could this be true? Had she married an impostor? Was she wedded to anything so awful as a heretic? Poor Sabine felt that her immortal soul was in danger.

There are some things which we will not believe even after we have received the clearest proofs of their truth. Sabine could not bring herself to believe that she had been duped by her own Bartie. That was impossible. The editor of that particular "Clergy List" was a stupid man, and poor Bartie had been forgotten. Still it was with no very easy heart that she went to bed that night. She could not get to sleep. Why was her husband so late? Was he beginning already to desert her in the second week of their marriage? Why does the candle go out just as she is in this unpleasant state of mind? and why will her thoughts keep reverting to that awful night—her bridal night at Dover? What did all this mean? Had she done wrong in marrying this man—who really seemed so good, so pure, so holy? If not, why were her dreams so unhappy, and what was the meaning of those anxious moments she felt occasionally? She was superstitious, she knew, but had she not had to do with facts and intensely unpleasant facts? For, for all that Bartlemy had urged to the contrary, she was positively certain that on the first night of her marriage she had seen in her room at the—. What? No! It was a night like this. The wind was sighing lugubriously in the trees of the Tuileries, and their rustling was not unlike the sound she had heard that fearful night of the waves lapping the shingly beach. Would that fearful figure appear again?

Sabine sat up in her bed with straining eyes and ears. All was quiet, save when some late cab rattled along the pavement. The night was wet and dark.

Sabine lay down again.

Why did he not come home? Was he angry with her? Had her cruel words of the morning hurt him so much that he had left her? Had she driven him to suicide, and would she find him on the morrow lying stiff and stark on one of the tables of the Morgue?

Poor Sabine! could she only have seen her lord and master then, sitting in the Café —, on the Boulevard des Italiens, surrounded by Hebes of every beauty and charm!

Bartlemy did not return home till early next morning, and went to sleep on the sofa in their sitting-room.

Sabine found him, when she got up, still asleep, lying fully dressed on the sofa, with his dripping umbrella still up over his head, his muddy boots on the silk cushion, and a bill for a champagne supper *en cabinet particulier* sticking in the button-hole of his overcoat.

This sight, coupled with the reminiscences of

other sights and general neglect, together with her awakened suspicions about his character, led Sabine to rouse him roughly, and then and there to tax him with his deceit.

The *reveille* of a night of debauch is not exactly the most fitting time to attack people on their lack of moral qualifications, and with a perverse and uncouth man like Hiram perhaps the worst time she could have chosen.

It would be too painful to the reader to relate verbatim what passed between the couple. Bartlemy was sullen and rude, and did not care to deny anything to the abusive and hysterical Sabine. They exchanged vituperations for some time, Sabine asserting that she had been wofully duped, that she never dreamt of marrying an American Skater (Shaker?), and affirming that she would very much like to see Bartlemy's funds. Her money was her own, and she meant to keep it; she was not going to keep a big man in sloth. Why did he call himself reverend if he was not so? He reverend, with his muddy boots on the silk cushions. How would he pay for them now they were spoilt? She knew that she wouldn't. Why did he not go back to his skaters? She would have a separation—and so on.

Bartlemy did not answer much during this tirade, and, with the exception of an occasional interpellated "Go on," kept remarkably quiet. As soon as she had finished, however, and was standing waiting for sufficient breath to carry on the attack, he rose clumsily from the sofa, and staggered towards her, caught her by the arm, and said in a voice hoarse with subdued passion, and in a tone of violent menace that made Sabine shake with fear—

"Look here, Mrs. Hiram, you have said enough. Don't say any more, I have the word now. You married me. I suppose you knew what you were doing. You can't plead the giddiness of youth, any way. Anyhow, I am your husband, and as such I have power over you. It depends on you whether I use this power or not to your discomfort. It does not matter now what I was before I married you. It does not matter a straw whether I told you a lie or not about my means and my profession. You force me to this confession. It does not pain me—it will pain you. I am not a clergyman of your Church ; I have officiated in a Shaker Chapel. I have no means whatever. I have nothing but my clothes and about eighteen francs. Yes, you wanted this, and you shall have it. Further, I married you because you have money, and my position was desperate. You shall not be spared a single detail. You have taxed me with a lie, I will give you the truth. I repeat, I married you for your money, and I mean to have the enjoyment of this money. What else did I marry you for ? Come, do you think you attracted me—charmed me? I have yet to discover the piquancy of wrinkles and grey hair. Now listen, I will come to a bargain with you. You are my wife, the wife, be it, of a penniless impostor. These are your own words. Nothing can undo that;

you are bound to me for life. I can force you to be with me always, day and night. Therefore it is your advantage to be on good terms with me. Let me have money, and keep quiet. We can settle down somewhere in England and have a comfortable life on your thousand a year. Defy me at your peril."

Stung to the quick in her pride, her avarice, her formal religion, maddened with shame and anger, the blood rushed to the unhappy woman's head in a red-hot torrent as she listened to the cold, shameless words addressed to her by a man with whom, by her own act and by her own free will, she was destined to pass the rest of her life.

Before he had half finished his speech Sabine fell heavily to the floor. She had fainted.

It is not with these two that my story has principally to deal, and it is with pleasure that I dismiss them for a time from its pages. A few short words concluding this chapter will suffice.

Sabine's fainting fit was followed by a violent attack of brain fever which kept her to her bed in the Hôtel Continental for many weeks. Her husband was most attentive to her and appeared unable to leave her bedside, or to give her into the sole charge of a nurse. He absolutely refused to allow either a French or an English nurse to attend to her, but secured the services of an old Greek woman, "who could not understand her nonsense."

Sabine never thoroughly recovered the effects of this illness. When she got better she seemed to have settled into a state of morbid hypochondriacism and moodiness.

As soon as she was well enough to be moved her husband took her to England, and hiring a small cottage on the Devonshire coast, installed her there. He did not trouble her much with his company, but was continually going away to London. Sabine still kept a rigid hand over her cash-box and Hiram had great difficulty in getting money from her. On such occasions, after violently disputing with his wife, he would refer in private to a dirty and worn letter which he carried about with him, the perusal of which seemed to put him in a state of doubt and hesitation.

Now back, as fast as thought can carry us, to the glorious South.

CHAPTER VII.

AMBITION AND LOVE.

THE Baroness de Bienaimée was a lover of all true manliness and of chivalrous deeds, and was so pleased with the account that the Chevalier de la Vigne had given of Charles's behaviour on the night of their return from the Toledo Lacrymæ Christi depôt, that she gave him to understand that he was always welcome at the Villa Dresda, so that Charles went as often as he could manage to do so, consistent with his idea of conventionality.

Herbert, who was financially independent, was so pleased with Italy and enjoyed the society of Charles and his new friends, the Mertons, so much, that he determined to stay on at Sorrento indefinitely as to time. He had also, through the introduction of Charles, the entry to the Villa Dresda, but, to tell the truth, he preferred the society of the Mertons. It had not taken long before he had learnt to admire the gentle beauty and amiability of Mildred. The warm South soon fans admiration into the flame of love, and scarcely a month had passed before Herbert began to feel that life without Mildred was not what life should be.

But Mildred was not ready to return his love, even had she known it. She was but a child, and having known sorrow and bereavement, in which she had been comforted by the society of her kind and amiable brother, she clung to him with a grateful love and could never think of leaving him.

There existed, however, a very friendly feeling between the three Americans, and Herbert was nearly always in the society of John Merton. At first their conversation had chiefly turned on the curious mistake that had brought their acquaintance about, and from Herbert John had learnt the whole story, and shared in his indignation, and sympathised with him in his sorrow. Their first meeting was often the subject of much pleasantry between the two young men, who never could decide who got the best of the physical encounter, each yielding the other the palm.

Even gentle Mildred learnt to laugh at the story retold, though she affirmed, that even now that Dr. Toogood's villany was exposed, she could not quite banish the affectionate remembrance she had of him, whom she had always looked upon as a benefactor, and who, bad though his motives might have been, had been the means of bringing her once more into the arms of her dear old mother.

Although Charles had now the opportunity of seeing Euphrosyne every day, and thus an excellent chance of pushing his suit, he did not progress very well.

Euphrosyne seemed to him to be interested in him out of sympathy with his literary tastes and knowledge, but that was all.

The Duke di Caserta did not often visit the Villa Dresda. He once told Charles the reason. He was paying his addresses to the daughter of a nobleman who lived at Florence, and frequently left Naples for that purpose.

Euphrosyne was very sad at this. She did so want to have him near her, to see him, to hear him laugh, to listen to his words, to hang on his sturdy arm.

It was one glorious evening, the sun had set in all its splendour behind the purple islands, and Charles was sitting with the two girls, Bianca and Euphrosyne, on the seaward terrace of the Villa Dresda.

They had asked him to read to them; he had been reading a French translation of Goethe, and they were talking about what he had read.

"How true are those lines," said Euphrosyne, "of Goethe's, that ambition cannot go hand in hand with love, and that ambition outstrides its gentler companion. Is it not so, Signor Carlo?"

"Signorina," answered Charles, blushing, "I do not know. I did not like the lines myself. I can fancy no greater happiness for a man than to fight his way through the world side by side with a woman he loves, to share his trouble with her, and to share his glory and success when the struggle is over."

"Oh, yes," said Bianca, impetuously, with a light coming into her flashing eyes, "I think so, too. How happy that woman must be. Happier than the Spartan mother who gave her son his shield. She stayed at home while her son was on the battle-field, but in the struggle with the world the wife stands at the warrior's right hand, and shares with him she loves the brunt of the battle, encourages him, allures him on to greater bravery, and sweetens with her company the pleasure of the victory."

"No," said Euphrosyne. "No, I do not think I should be happy thus. Is not a woman's love the ultimate of man's happiness? Do not men say so? Then why should a man possessing this strive for worldly success? An ambitious man would make me unhappy. He would first tell me that I was all in all to him, and then he would set about to gain a further happiness. No, to rest for ever with him—that were my happiness."

"Not mine," said Bianca, with impetuosity. "Not mine. I could not love a slothful man, a lotus-eater. We have no longer mailed knights to do valiant deeds to prove their love for us, but men can still prove that they think no sacrifice, no labour too great to be made for us, not on the tourney field, be it, but in the harder arena of life."

Charles, who had listened with great attention to what the two girls had said, turned his eyes on them.

Bianca was standing with some of the enthusiasm of her words expressed in her whole form. Euphrosyne was sitting at her feet in an attitude of devotional repose. She was thinking of Arnolfo. Bianca was dreaming of the man who would invite her some day to stand by his side and fight the battle of the world with him.

Euphrosyne was dreaming of the happiness of a life of eternal rest; a life void of struggle and movement; a life full of poetry, music, sunlight and flowers, of life, of love, love given, love returned in fullest measure.

Bianca spoke next; turning to Charles—

"And you, Signor Carlo? You are a man. What will your life be? Have you a fight to fight, or are you going to rest?"

She fixed a curious glance on him, and with fire lighting in her eyes awaited his answer.

"Rest?" cried Charles, rising to his feet and throwing out his arms. "Rest? No, lady, if ever man had work to do it is I. Rest! while a shame cankers my innermost soul. Rest! while I walk a pariah among lesser men. Rest! while I grind my teeth at an unmerited reproach. Rest? No lady, there is no rest to me. If I had the eternal force, the restless activity of those blue waves, I might still despair of doing what I have to do. For me there will be no rest till it is done, or the Fates achieve their injustice, and I am lain where I can work no more."

Bianca never took her eyes off him while he was speaking. Euphrosyne, too, startled by the intense energy and passion expressed in his voice, was listening intently.

Charles continued—

"I have to smite the world on the cheek and

say, 'Thou hast lied.' I have to raise myself from the shade and make myself prominent among men. I have to climb a hill, barred at each step of my rugged path by falsehood, by envy, by contempt, by prejudice. I have to fight against all the world; I have a bitterer fight to fight against myself. For," continued he, turning to Euphrosyne, in a tone full of love and admiration, "there are times when I think as you do, Signorina; times when all seems to invite to repose; times when all is so beautiful that it seems folly to think of the foolish world; times when the struggle with such an opponent seems unworthy; times when love of one beautiful, pure angel seems enough. Then it is that I have to fight against myself."

"Why!" said Euphrosyne; "would you not be happy thus?"

"No, Signorina, the woman who marries me must not be wedded to a living reproach. There are things in this world which nothing can undo. A murderer may expiate his crime, a renegade recant his heresy, but from the shame of the sins of our fathers there is no deliverance. But there shall be a deliverance. And it is to do what even I, who hope to do it, just called impossible, that I can take no rest."

The two girls looked at each other in silence. There was a pause; all were busy with their thoughts.

Charles broke the silence by saying—

"Excuse me, ladies, if I have talked too loudly things which cannot interest you. They interest me too much, I know, not to appear selfish. They are of me, my being."

With this he bade them good-bye. Euphrosyne kept his hand in hers some time, then she said—

"Do not be unhappy; Carlo; is not the world too beautiful? The world of God, not the world of men. Men have always been cruel, at least some. You will tell me some day what your grief is, will you not?"

Charles bent over her little hand and kissed it. He then gave his hand to Bianca. She turned away and released it without a pressure.

He then went, but before he had reached the gate he heard a nimble step behind him. It was Bianca. Her cheek was flushed, her whole face excited, and her eyes were flashing wildly.

"I did not bid you a good good-night just now," she said hurriedly. "I have come to say it now. I was thinking."

"You are very good," said Charles.

"I was thinking that to you nothing should be impossible. I am as excited as you were. I never heard a man talk as you did. Remember, to the brave nothing is impossible. I do not know your sorrow, but I saw you wince when you were speaking, and I know it must be great. You will fight well, will you not? and now a better good-night."

Charles raised her hand to his lips and bowed. He went on his way, but looking back he saw her white form standing in the midst of the gleaming foliage, her hand raised aloft as if motioning him forward, forward!

CHAPTER VIII.

THE CHEVALIER'S WOOING.

A FEW days after Charles' conversation on the stirring questions of ambition and love, he received a visit at the Grande Sentinelle from his friend the Chevalier de la Vigne, who had moved from the Villa Castiglione to the luxurious Hotel Tramontano at Sorrento.

When Charles asked him the reason of his leaving his comfortable quarters at Pausilipo, the little Chevalier burst out into a storm of reproach against the unhappy Castiglione.

"A most unheard-of outrage," said he. "Five nights ago, while I was peacefully sitting in my room I heard a knock at the door, and the secretary of the villa made his appearance. He had the barefaced audacity to ask me if I had any objection to leave the house at once, adding that it did not matter whether I paid my bill or not immediately, adding with the most consummate insolence that it might not be convenient to me to do so. I asked if he had perhaps not been dining too heavily. He is of the Israelitic persuasion, and no morsel had passed his lips, so help him Moses. I then asked him what he meant by telling me to go, adding that I had no intention of leaving; and, as to my solvency, referring him to Messrs. Altier and Cie. He said he felt sorry, it was not a question of personality, but Signore Castiglione, who had been a long time in treaty with three Russian princes with a view to letting his villa for three months, had that evening received a telegram closing the bargain, and all *pensionnaires* had been asked to go. I said, 'Damn the three Russian princes, I am comfortable here, and, with the exception of certain eccentricities of certain of the ladies who dine at the *table d'hôte*, very well contented with the arrangements.' But it appeared that I could not stay, and so I left that night. It does not speak well for the discrimination of M. Castiglione to prefer three shoddy Russians to a de la Vigne. To punish him I wrote to the editor of the *Pungolo*, on the 'Insolence of Italian Hotel-keepers,' but that ruffian had the courage to tell me that he could not insert my letter unless I paid for it as an advertisement, by postage stamps or post-office order. If that is the way they behave under a monarchy, I shall certainly lend my support to the Italia Irridenta party."

"Well," said Charles, "there is one comfort, you are now near Mademoiselle de Bienaimée."

"A great comfort that is," answered the Chevalier with a doleful tone. "In spite of my most elegant toilets and the services of a transcendant hairdresser from Naples I make no progress with the lady. She seems a marble statue; and I did not come here to investigate art. I am seriously thinking of going back to Paris and taking up my *liaison* with la Catalani of the Hippodrome, though she costs me awful sums, especially in paying the managerial fines for her."

This was good news to Charles, who, however, did not dare to encourage the Frenchman in his proposal for fear of betraying himself.

"But come," added the Chevalier, "I have an invitation for you. We are to lunch at the Villa Dresda, and I am really going to do my best to-day to ingratiate myself with Phrosyne. My uncle will be so angry if I return to Paris with nothing but a few cakes of Naples soap, very nice soap by the way, after all this most Quixotic adventure of mine. Now be a good fellow and help me in this matter."

"How can I?" said Charles, with an unintentional *double entendre.*

"When you think I have made an impression, just nudge me; it will give me courage to go on. We must manage to sit next to each other. And look here at this paper. I have arranged some little *jeux d'esprit* to bring in, in a quiet way, into the conversation. You see I have written them out. There is one from Moliére, one I heard at the Palais-Royal theatre, a few from Brillat-Savarin, and one, by myself, quite original. It took me eight days to perfect, and when I told it to Catalani she said she only hoped she would not remember it at the Hippodrome that night, or she would surely fall off her saddle. She added, though I confess I don't see the point of it, that the *boite* was close enough already."

Equipped with all these weapons of love did the

natty little Chevalier set forth to the Villa Dresda, accompanied by Charles. The latter was not in good spirits; how could he be, walking side by side with a rival, who, although excessively foolish and absurd, was from his position, his birth, and his claim of kinship with Euphrosyne, by no means a despicable one.

Arrived at the villa, they were received on the terrace by the Baroness. She received Charles most cordially, and told him that he would find Bianca in the arbour, and that she wanted to show him some drawings she had made.

Greeting the Chevalier, the Baroness had an expression of amusement, such as one sees on the faces of good-natured elderly people when speaking to a child. Truly the Chevalier was amusing. As soon as he had reached the terrace, and was in sight of the lady, he had made his first little bow, which he performed by drawing himself up stiffly and slowly making a right angle of himself, the middle of his back being the apex thereof. This he repeated three times, advancing between each bow with a little mincing step. Had the Baroness not been the courtly, well-bred lady that she was she could not have helped laughing.

He immediately asked how her daughter was, and the Baroness said she was well. He then paused, he wanted to ask where she was, but did not want to appear too pressing.

To tell the truth, the Baroness did not look with a favourable eye on the little Chevalier's suit. She had her own ideas on the subject of manliness, and wanted to see her wedded to the most perfect man she could find. Still, though the contemplation of a union between Euphrosyne and de la Vigne caused her no pleasurable feelings, she was too just and honest to attempt to interfere in any way with her daughter's inclinations, or to force her one way or the other.

Indeed, though she wished Euphrosyne to marry eventually, lest the ancient line of the illustrious Bienaimées should die out, she did not recognise any immediate necessity for a step which would separate her from her darling child. If she entertained the idea of anyone as a son-in-law, she decidedly inclined to the manly, strong, and handsome di Caserta. She knew that Euphrosyne admired him, but she did not understand his feelings towards Euphrosyne. He appeared indifferent, but well the Baroness knew that men often don the mask of indifference to conceal feelings of which they affect to feel ashamed.

She resolved, however, to let the Chevalier have his full chance, and so she told him that he would find Euphrosyne in the arbour with Bianca.

The Chevalier accordingly proceeded to the moss-grown rockery that was called the arbour. He found the two girls busy showing Charles some drawings they had made. Bianca's were all illustrations of her fancies of chivalrous knights and doughty warriors. Euphrosyne's were sketches of the beautiful nature of the Bay of Naples, of flowers and trees, views of the sea, pleasant little rills trickling from some age-greened boulder on the hills behind, and in all her drawings was expressed the artist's love of sunlight and repose. Bianca's illustrated the moving incidents of romance, the moonlit battle-field, the tourney, the fight against dragons and similar subjects; Bianca drew movement and tragedy, Euphrosyne repose and peace.

Charles was in one of his quietest moods, and had for some time abandoned his ambitious yearnings, so that he found more pleasure in the quiet harmonies of Euphrosyne, than in the wild designs of Bianca. When he was asked, therefore, by the Chevalier which of the class of the drawings he preferred, he said—

"La Signora Euphrosyna's. They suit my mood. They all suggest quiet, repose, happiness."

"Tityre, tu recubans, &c.," put in the Chevalier.

"Why," said Bianca, pleading her cause with fire, "did you not say that for you there should be no rest, and do you recant now? Does not movement and battle urge you on, does not the contemplation of the beauties of repose invite you to pernicious sloth? Pernicious, for you said that you had the world to smite on the cheek."

"What a very *outrée* proposal," said the Chevalier.

"It is one of my relapses to-day, Signorina," answered Charles.

"The ambitious should suffer no relapses," said

Bianca, scornfully. "I despise the gladiator who sleeps at the entrance of the arena, putting off the struggle he is bound to undergo."

"Do not talk about arenas," said the Chevalier, "for you bring to my mind that very unpleasant day I spent at Pompeji. Some very vigorous Englishmen who were staying at the Villa Castiglione, the manager of which establishment is, in parenthesis, unacquainted with the rudiments of politeness, got me to accompany them to Pompeji. I shall never forget the discomfort I suffered. The dust, the heat! And there was nothing to see after all. I felt like Tantalus all the time I was promenading the streets. The guide would lead us up to an old ruin and say to me, dying of thirst and hunger, 'This, gentlemen, was the shop of a fruiterer. The most luscious melons, the coolest of grapes, the juiciest of pomegranates, may be supposed to have lain on this slab.' Or, leading us to another tumble-down hut, he would remark that a perfumer had formerly exercised his profession there. My remark that it was a pity that no perfumes had escaped the lava to scent the air, in lieu of a peculiar, strong smell of garlic, was received by the guide as an insult. Not content with dragging me off my legs, through all the narrow streets of this town, I was obliged to follow my friends a long way, till we got to the arena. I hope no gladiator ever suffered as much as I did from weariness. When some sturdy Briton suggested Herculaneum, I attributed it to the playful irony which distinguishes the countrymen of

Shakespeare. It subsequently transpired, however, that he was in full earnest."

During this speech Bianca and Charles exchanged glances more than once. Bianca's eyes turning with amusement from the Chevalier, rested with a look of pity on Euphrosyne, who was listening patiently to her cousin's talk.

When he had finished, and was refreshing himself after his exertion by fanning himself with his scented handkerchief, Euphrosyne said with a little laugh—

"Well, Monsieur Alphonse, I am sorry you do not like Pompeji, because mamma wants me to go there, and thought you could escort us."

"I would do any service for a lady," said the Chevalier, bowing, "even this disagreeable one. I shall have much pleasure in escorting you to Pompeji."

"Oh, do not put yourself out, dear Cavaliere," said Bianca, hastily. "We would not for the world expose you to fatigue, and, as you find this service a disagreeable one, we must find another escort."

The Chevalier was heartily relieved; he bowed.

"Perhaps," said Euphrosyne, glancing at Charles, "il Signor Inglese would be so kind?"

"Mademoiselle," answered Charles, "nothing would make me happier, but I will not infringe on the privileges and rights of this gentleman."

"Privileges?" said Euphrosyne.

"Rights?" echoed Bianca.

The poor little Chevalier looked at Charles as

much as to say, "Well, that is your way of furthering my suit, is it?"

Lunch was then announced, and during it the subject of their proposed visit to the disinterred town was discussed. Indeed, it occupied the whole conversation, and the Chevalier did not get one opportunity of shining. It was only while coffee was being handed round that he saw his chance, and before losing it, he burst, without any introduction, into the following.

"One day, at Naples, I saw a man selling cocoa nuts, and so I asked the man,

"'Comment appelle-t'on cela?'

"He answered—

"'Non si pela, ma si rompe.'

"'Comment?' said I.

"'Non con mano, ma con martello,' answered he.

"'Je ne vous comprends pas,' said I.

"'Eh,' said he, 'se non lo comprate voi, lo compra un altro.'

"Then he turned to a neighbouring orange-vendor and added—

"'Well, at least, one can understand these Germans.'"

Euphrosyne was perhaps the only one who had listened; she laughed heartily.

This so encouraged the Chevalier that he began to tell a dubious Palais-Royal witticism, but one reproachful glance of the Baroness' was enough to silence him. He understood Euphrosyne as little as Charles did.

It was then arranged that Charles should accompany the three ladies to Pompeji, leaving Sorrento the next day at about four, in time to catch the 5.30 p.m. train from Castellamare.

Very happy at this prospect, he returned home; happier still because before leaving the Villa Dresda Euphrosyne had asked him if he would like to take one of her drawings with him to keep.

"You are a poet," she said. "I see that, and you will find beauty in this poor little sketch of mine. You see the subject was rather a sad one, a bunch of flowers thrown into the cruel salt sea. I saw it the other day. The flowers had lost their fragrance and were withering in the biting waters. Take it as an emblem if you like; an emblem of a beautiful life thrown away in the bitterness of the world, or of the blight of a searing ambition on a mind made to enjoy the beautiful."

Charles took it, and Bianca, who was standing by, said—

"I will put a piece of paper round it, it will get soiled with the dust if you carry it thus."

When he got home and undid the cover he found not one but two pictures. The other was signed Bianca.

It represented a knight departing armed for battle from his castle. Under the gateway stood a lady, with her hand raised aloft, as if motioning him onward and forward to victory. Her expression was beautifully studied, her face denoted a victory over the pain she felt at losing her dear lord, and yet an expression of courage, and the smile of a triumph anticipated rested on her features.

The handful of sweet flowers, thirsting in the pitiless salt waters of the cruel, devouring sea, and the knight sped on his way by his ambitious lady to conquer or to die, were they emblems? were they tokens?

CHAPTER IX.

A LETTER FROM AMERICA.

It was just after dinner; Herbert had gone upstairs to play a game of bezique with John Merton, and Charles was sitting over his coffee with a "little white enemy" between his teeth. He was interrupted in a pleasant meditation by a waiter, who brought him a delicate little note and two letters.

The note was from Euphrosyne. When the woman we love first writes to us, how minutely we weigh each word, striving to find in each conventional word of polite endearment something we can construe into an expression of a predilection on her part towards us. The note was short, written in polite Italian. It ran thus—

"Splendid Mr. Charles,

"Could your friend, Mr. Lovell, accompany us to-morrow to Pompeji? Mamma thought he might like to come, and we should be glad of his company.

"Your most devoted,

"Euphrosyne."

"Why has she written in Italian?" thought Charles with a sigh of regret. "Why did she not show me in English what she thinks her relation to me is?" For Charles well knew that the words "splendid" and "most devoted" are in use between the greatest strangers in courteous Italy. For my part, I should be better pleased to be told by a pretty girl that she was "most devoted" to me in hyperbolical Italian than to hear that she remained "mine sincerely" in formal English.

One of the letters was for Charles. It came from Dorothy. She told him that she had been very ill, nigh unto death, but that the little woman was better now, and could get about comfortably. She begged him to write to her, for, as she said, "Who in the world, except the mother you have lost, has ever cared for you as I do?"

The other letter was in a mourning envelope, and came from America. It was not for Charles at all. It was addressed to Herbert Lovell, at Leipzic, and had been forwarded.

Charles took the note and the letter up to Merton's apartment. He gave them to Herbert and waited to hear his answer. Mildred brought him some coffee, and John, who had heard his praises sung repeatedly by Herbert, reproached him for not coming oftener.

Charles said he had so much work to do that he could not well manage to pay any visits.

"Visits? Mr. Hauberk. Please don't use such very formal words. We live in the same house, and we ought to be good friends. No, I don't want you to leave cards on me at intervals, but to come and see us, and play cards, and hear Mildred sing, and then we would come and see you."

"I regret," said Charles, "that I cannot avail

myself very often of the pleasures of the interesting programme you hold out. I have infinite work to do, and I am sure if I came often I should come too often, and then my work would be neglected. But, Herbert, what is the matter?"

Herbert had read his letter in silence, and at the end had risen to his feet pale and excited.

"I have bad news, very bad news, from New York. My step-father is dead."

"Your father is dead?" exclaimed John and Mildred rising to their feet.

"My poor friend," continued John, taking hold of Herbert's hand, while Mildred timidly took the other. "Your father dead?"

"No, that grief has passed long ago. I don't remember it. It is my step-father, who was as kind to me as any father could be, who is dead."

"Sit down again and get calm," said Mildred in a voice full of compassion.

"I am quite calm," said Herbert, with a grateful glance at the girl. "I have not realised it yet. My mother is in the greatest grief. He was the best of men."

Sister and brother both did their best to comfort their stricken friend, and Charles too helped in this ministration. By-and-bye Herbert said he would rather retire, he would feel better alone. Then bidding his friends good-night, with many thanks, he walked slowly and sorrowfully out of the room.

"Poor fellow," said John.

"Poor, poor boy," said Mildred, "and yet a

brave boy too; he bears it well, strongly, manfully, does he not?"

"I never doubted that Herbert Lovell would lack in manliness at any time, or under any circumstances," said John with warm affection.

When Charles went to bed that night he found on his table Euphrosyne's note, Herbert's letter, and a pencil line from his friend, telling him to read the letter, and adding that he could not go out on a pleasure-trip at present.

(*Copy of a letter from Mrs. Dixon to her son Herbert Lovell.*)

"New York.

"My Dearest Herbert,

"When last I wrote, I told you that your papa was ailing and now I have to tell you the fearful news that he is dead. He died yesterday afternoon, quite peacefully and conscious to the end. Almost his last words were, 'Give my dear love to my boy and tell him what I regret, next to leaving you, is not to see him again. He was always a good, true, honest, affectionate lad, and a great comfort to all of us.' Shortly afterwards he tried to write you a few lines, expressing his love, but his pen fell from his hand, and a few minutes afterwards he left us.

"I am in the greatest affliction, and miss you more than anything. You alone could bring me comfort in this terrible sorrow.

"I cannot speak decisively about my plans for the future. Your papa has left everything he possesses between us; and his partner, Mr. Cooper, who has been most kind, has arranged to settle all the money matters, and to pay for Mr. Dixon's share in the brewery.

"I think it very probable that I shall come over to Europe, not to England, I cannot breathe English air, but perhaps I shall settle down in Italy.

"However, I will write more fully to-morrow, I am so weary with grief that I can write no more to-day. My dear, dear boy, take many, many kisses from your poor mother, and believe ever and always,

"Your most loving mother,

"DORA DIXON.

"P.S.—I forgot. Just as he was dying, I bent over him to take a last kiss from his dear lips, and I heard him say these last words, with almost his last breath. 'Dora, forgive poor Esther, love from me.' If ever I bore my poor sister any ill-will, this dying prayer of a man whom I have loved and respected so many years, would more than atone for any fault of hers. Now good-bye, my dear son, you are all to me now."

Next morning, Charles went into Herbert's room to see how he was bearing his sorrow. He found him sitting up in bed, reading a letter.

"How do you feel, this morning?" asked Charles.

"I did not sleep much last night," answered Herbert. "I have been thinking of the dead man that is gone. What a comfort his blessing is to me. It is for my dear mother that I feel more than for myself. Tell me, Charles, did you love *your* mother dearly?"

"But for the fact that I am alive, I have no proof that I ever had a mother. No, I have no reason to cherish her memory. Her legacy to me was one of grief, of tears, of reproach. I never knew her, my happiness is there," was the bitter reply of Charles.

Herbert looked at him affectionately and sorrowfully, then he said—

"I have received another letter this morning. My mother appears decided not to stay in New York, and wishes to come over to Europe. She will not go to England."

"I noticed that she said that she could not breathe English air. Is she delicate?"

"No," said Herbert, with a smile. "Physically she has no objection to England. She must have suffered much there. She has often said that she could not rest in an English grave."

"Do you know why?" asked Charles.

"No; my mother's past is a profound secret to me, she has never told me about herself or her youth, and of my father I know nothing. True it is I have never questioned her much, she appeared to dislike questions on the subject. I have a vague impression that he was a lawyer in London, but that is all. I have lost a dear father in Mr. Dixon, that is what I know."

"When does your mother intend to come over, do you know?"

"I should think in a few months; she does not give a date in this letter, but she says, 'I do not like the idea of remaining in New York, the society here is not very tasteful to me,' and adds that she has almost made up her mind to come to Italy. I wrote last night to tell her where I was, and I shall hear from her in a few weeks. She will have quite made up her mind by then. How glad I am that I received this painful news here, where I have such dear friends, and not alone in Leipzic. What nice people those Mertons are!"

"Yes," said Charles, "they appear a very worthy, respectable young couple. I regret that I am unable to cultivate their nearer acquaintance."

"Why is that?"

"Because it is of vital importance to me to be very careful in forming any connections. I do not know if you take my meaning, but I must not get to know people who, though excellent in their sphere, might eventually be a bar to my progress."

Herbert looked at him sorrowfully, and holding out his hand, said—

"My dear Charles, will the prize when you have won it be worth all the sacrifice you are making? I do not exactly know what you are striving after, but I know that, now-a-days, rewards come late, and will a bitter youth be atoned for by a successful old age? When you have gained what you desire, will that counterbalance the pleasures you have lost? Will it bring back all the warm beauties of life, the bright flowers of life which you have trodden beneath your feet in your hasty path-taking towards the goal?"

Ah Euphrosyne! Euphrosyne! The sweet flowers dripping with the bitter brine of the sea. How eloquently they spoke to Charles now.

But he steeled his heart, and refused to tarry by the pleasant wayside, on, on, along the dusty road to the ultimate dim thule of his ambition.

So he answered, with somewhat of a cold rebuke in his tone. "I do not quite understand you, Herbert, everybody has his place in society. I, mine; the Mertons, theirs. We will keep them, if you please. They do not affect in the least any proposition I have made to myself, any plan I may have arranged for the future."

"Well," said Herbert cheerfully, "my dear fellow, of course you know best. And I hope you will have a very pleasant day of it. You must bring back a long account from Pompeji."

"I am so sorry that you cannot come," said Charles.

"I could come, only I think I ought to devote this day, at least, to the memory of the dead. I should not feel happy if I spent the morrow of my receiving the news of his death in pleasure-taking."

"Of course not," said Charles. "I never meant to suggest such a thing."

He then bąde his friend good-bye, and was going to leave the room when Herbert said—

"Oh, there is one thing I forgot. There is an English paper lying there. Take it, it may interest your friends. There is a long account of a new French play in it."

Charles took the paper, and bidding Herbert farewell, went back to his books.

It had been arranged that he should lunch at the Villa Dresda, spend the afternoon there, and take the ladies to Pompeji in the evening.

Lunch passed very pleasantly; the girls were in good spirits at the prospect of seeing so interesting a sight, and Charles was quite happy in the presence of Euphrosyne.

After lunch the girls asked Charles to read to them; and Bianca further suggested that they should take the boat and row into the shade of a cliff, and then Signor Carlo could read to them.

This was done, and Charles took Beranger's poems with him to read.

But the girls soon complained they did not want poetry, had he not anything interesting?

"Oh, yes," said Charles, "I have an English newspaper here, there is plenty of interest in that. Shall I read you the police news. Here's an interesting account of a fearful double murder and suicide at Clapham, an audacious burglary at Putney, a wonderful pickpocketing case at Parson's Green, and a blazing fire at Kensington."

"No," said Bianca, laughing, "is there nothing about art in that big sheet, that looks for all the world like a sail?"

"Yes," said Charles, "there is an account of a new play at the 'Français.' It seems interesting."

He then read it to them. When he had finished, it was time to go home, so he folded up his paper to put it into his pocket. While he was doing this his eye fell on a prominently placed advertisement. He read it carelessly. It ran—

NOTICE.—Would the lady who helped a poor girl at the Grosvenor Hotel, in October last, kindly communicate with the lawyer who called on her on that occasion. By doing so she will greatly oblige. Sister's address not known.

Had Charles looked a little lower down he would have seen this other advertisement:—

£100 REWARD.—Whoever can give information as to the whereabouts of Esther Lovell, lately in America, and last seen in London, will receive the above reward. Also, should this meet the eye of Esther Lovell, she is earnestly entreated to communicate with the advertiser at once.—John George Bennett, Lincoln's Inn, London.

Charles did not row fast enough for the girls, who were anxious to get home in order to get ready for their excursion. Bianca had a famous idea.

"Let us take his paper, Phrosyne, and make a sail of it. I will hold two ends and you the other. Look, we can do it so."

What a pretty picture they made, these two girls, holding the mimic sail, merrily laughing as the boat sped its way through the blue waters; the fearless Bianca erect, and the timid Euphrosyne crouching in the boat, with all her brown hair blowing wildly in the wind, flushed with the sea breeze, and merrily laughing to think that she was helping the boat along.

Just before they got home the wind grew stronger, and a sudden gust tore the sail out of the girls' hands. It blew into the sea and was lost.

CHAPTER X.

THE CITY OF THE DEAD.

FEW reminiscences were pleasanter to Charles in after life than that of his first visit to Pompeji. At four o'clock that afternoon the Baroness's barouche was ready to take them to Castellamare, Charles sat opposite to Euphrosyne the whole time, and this was enough to make him very happy. They were all so merry, and even the stately mother unbent, and joined freely in the cheerful conversation. Euphrosyne was radiant with smiles, and Bianca, prattling all the time, a charming Lalage.

The drive from Sorrento to Castellamare is considered one of the most beautiful in the world. The road lies straight at first, and runs through several quaint and beautiful villages, with the white walls of the cottages rising from the midst of gardens radiant with all colours, with picturesque villas dotted here and there, and every now and then some lofty church raising its gilded cupola into the transparent air; then through some old market place, which for centuries has been the meeting place of the bronzed and black-bearded idlers of the village, the rendezvous of gossipy, white-tunicked women; past the villages, along the mountain side, over gorges, green with luxuriant foliage, through the gleaming pearly dust—for even the dust is beautiful in Italy; and then slowly winding up the promontorial mountain side, to descend on the yon side, through fresh beauties, to the level of the blue sea, to Castellamare. At every point the view presents new beauties, but nowhere perhaps is it so remarkable as when the top of the promontory is reached, before the road bends inwards and downwards to Castellamare. From here the whole table land of Sorrento and Massa is descried. The chief effect in colour is an intensely beautiful green, broken here and there with the red and white roofs of houses, or the flush of some oleander in bloom. Behind this wavy mass of spangled green rise high mountains, covered with silvery olive trees, deep green myrtles, looping vines, or the little white huts of the coloni. To the right, the sea gleaming like a mass of silver and azure threads entwined, moving beneath the faint breath of some breeze balmy with a thousand scents. Beyond, the islands of Procida, the brown lava-strewn heights of Ischia, the low-lying peninsula of Posilipo. Over all, the glorious Italian sky, dancing with warmth, and apparently aglow with pleasure.

It was at this point that the Baroness bade the coachman stop, and for a few minutes the party gave themselves the pleasure of looking at the exquisite panorama. While thus occupied a wandering tramp, of the Italian gipsy type, went by with his wife. A little while afterwards, his son, a sturdy little fellow of about eight or nine years, came past the carriage. Seeing gentlefolks, he stopped and, putting out his hand, said in a voice half pleading, half-threatening, "Muori di fam;' 'muori di fam,' 'no sold,' 'no sold.'"

Then, seeing that they gave him nothing, he raised his stick, and placed it against his shoulder like a gun, and stood in this menacing attitude as if about to fire on them. The pose was a very graceful one, and the attitude, dress, and expression were strikingly picturesque. This little boy, a mere child, browned by the sun, standing with his little naked feet and legs white with dust, clad in a blue shirt, a ragged pair of corduroys, and a red rag twisted into his black hair, as an only protection against all the inclemencies of weather he might encounter in his wanderings. There was something interesting in this menace from so mere a child, conscious, as it were, of its strength and inured in the fatal knowledge of the weapons that the poor use against the rich, violence, brigandage, murder. The effect this little incident had on the different occupants of the barouche was diverse. Charles laughed, remarking, "The tiger's cub shows its teeth;" Euphrosyne looked interested in the pose; Bianca jumped out of the carriage, and lifting the ragged, dusty, little brigand into her arms, kissed him on both his ruddy cheeks; the Baroness acted most wisely, perhaps, bidding the coachman give the boy a few soldi, with which the child departed, not with an air of gratitude but of triumph, as if he had battled and won.

As soon as the carriage started again, Bianca said to Charles, laying emphasis on each word—

"I like that boy. He will be a man. He is a man. He meets disappointment with the point of the sword. He cannot even conceive defeat. Yet a few soldi were the object of his ambition, and he gained them. In the same way, little will lie beyond his power of obtaining what he wants."

"If he does not previously find his way to Nesida," said Charles.

Bianca answered nothing but lay back in the carriage, and from time to time threw a keen searching glance at Charles, who was busily talking to Euphrosyne.

They then drove on without interruption to Castellamare, passing by gardens of orange trees, fig, pomegranate and arbutus trees, through vineyards, by olive-tree plantations, or by uncultivated mountain sides where the myrtle and mastich-tree luxuriated.

At Castellamare they took the train to Pompeji, and reached the little station about six o'clock. A walk of about two hundred yards led them to the entrance of the town of the dead; here they were supplied with a guide, and, full of anticipation and interest, they passed through the Porta Marina into the silent city.

One enters Pompeji full of interest and excitement, one leaves it, depressed, heavy at heart, melancholy and mournful. Here, more than elsewhere, does a man, though confident of his strength, recognise how feeble he is opposed to the Titan sisters, Nature and Time. He sees here the traces of all the fruits of human energy, art, religion, commerce, pleasure, vice, all effaced, and plunged in eternal silence. The once busy shops, the theatres, the amphitheatre, the temples of the gods, the forum where eloquent voices once enthralled the eager listeners, the market places, once thronged with wrangling merchants, are all given over to a pulseless, voiceless void. *Thou shalt perish, Son of Woman. Ye shall perish ye gods of man,* is what each silent wall seems to bear on it in flaming letters, written by the same hand that hurled the ominous MENE, MENE, TEKEL UPHARSIN at the drunken lord of the Babylonians.

Where are now the men who paced these narrow streets, unremembered save by their footprints on the yielding pavement? Where are now the gods that were worshipped then? Does their presence still haunt the naked precincts of their desolate temples, waiting for a sacrifice that will never be made, for an oblation eternally postponed?

Before reflections like these do not the same questions arise with regard to us, of this day? When time has buried us beneath a pall that cannot be removed, like the shroud that lay over the town of the Pompejians, what trace will there be of us, and, infinitely more awful question, where will be the culture of the gods we now worship? Will not their fall be a more terrible one than this, for while we worship the emblems of eternal love and purity, the Pompejians bent their knees to the impersonations of lust, theft, and murder. We start back horror-stricken before the proofs that this town affords of the fearful degeneracy and immorality of its age; are we better to-day, or do not our towns contain vices more hideous than these, crimes more appalling?

It may be that thoughts like these kept Charles busy, for he was silent while they walked through the ghostly precincts of the town.

No one spoke much saving the guide, who seemed wound up, and unwinding a flow of talk.

At each spot Charles tried to imagine the people who had once walked the place. In the Forum, the stately white-bearded senators gravely discussing the news from Rome; in the Temple of Venus young lovers blushingly bringing offerings to their patron, wooing her favour for their love; in the Tribunals the venal magistrates dispensing justice, if it was paid for; below in the vaults the poor debtors, or prisoners of no account, trembling.

"Cave Canem" was the inscription, so told them the guide, written in Mosaic on the threshold of the House of the Tragic Poet, which they passed on their way to the Thermæ. "Cave Canem," was it an omen? For, standing in the atrium of this ruin, Charles was startled to see no one of less importance than his old acquaintance of Moll's Coll., Oxford—Mangles Brewerides. Yes, it was Mangles, dazzling in a tweed suit of the most brilliant pattern, correctly got up as the Englishman on the Continent, with a blue gauze veil round his straw hat, an opera glass slung in a case by his side, a large green parasol, and, finest touch of all, a Baedeker in its flaring red back in his hand.

Cave Canem, by all means, thought Charles, as he hurried before the rest of the party into the retreat of the Thermæ, for of all persons, even were it not for the unpleasant relation which still existed between them, his unpaid debt, Mangles was the last person he wished to see. To have unpleasant things told about him to the Baroness, perhaps thereby to lose his acquaintance with them, to be held up a suspicious character, hiding under an alias, was not so much his reason for wishing to shun the young man, but being at Pompeji he would not, could not submit to have his mind thrown out of the poetical state that it was in by the venalities and vulgarisms of Mr. Mangles, and to carry away, not a serious, lasting impression of a melodious silence, but faint echoes of plebeian English phrases of conventional admiration, and of the distressing formulæ of his countrymen. How truly rural. How nice. Really, how interesting.

The house of the Tragic Poet is nearly opposite the Thermæ, and as Brewerides had the habit of speaking loud, all that he said was heard by Charles. His speech jarred on Charles's ear, strung to a delicate pitch by the melodious Italian of the guide, and the poetical Latinity suggested by the place.

"What d'yer call this? The Adrian, eh? Why Adrian? Was Adrian a tragic poet, and why did he keep a dog? A cave dog too. What's a cave dog? Who slept in those 'oles? Cubicules did yer say? Why Cubicules? And what poetry did he write, and did his dog disturb him? And where's the refreshments? I'm dry after this trotting. Chiefly beer and sugar line myself. Where's yer beer, and who brewed it? What was the dog's name? Nonkey Pisco. A rum name for a dog. Yes I hear. Nonkey Pisco. What breed? Oh! Nonkey Pisco too! Rum idea to call it after its breed. A sort of spaniel wolf-terrier. And where's the Amphitheatre? A'dear, how charming. Reely the view is fine. What's that island called? Nonkey Pisco too! Dear, dear," &c., &c.

Charles managed to escape Mangles, and did not meet him at all.

Their visit was drawing to a close. Passing back through the Forum Charles strayed away, unobserved by the watchful guide, into the temple of Venus. Ascending the steps, which lead from the basement to the real temple, Charles looked around; in front of him rose, lit by the rosy glow of the heavens, the Monte St. Angelo. All was hushed, and solemn in the approaching night.

Charles turned to the temple. On the altar where of yore so many trembling hands had laid their offerings to the foam-born goddess, sat two doves. Startled by his approach they rose, fluttered in the air, and settled down again on the broken coronal of a column.

A few wild flowers grew on the soil that lay

between the crannies of the stone. Charles picked these, and with uncovered head laid them on the votive stone.

It was thus Euphrosyne saw him. She, too, had come to take a last look at the temple of the Paphian queen.

He was standing there with his arms thrown out as if in supplication, his black hair floating out on the evening wind. In front of him the altar, and by his side the column, where sat emblems of true love, the bright-plumaged doves, and over all a perfect silence.

Euphrosyne stayed, one foot resting on the broken step, and the flush of the skies lighting up her face, regarding Charles.

At last she spoke—

"Signor Carlo, we are returning. Will you not come?"

He turned and blushed, then slowly descended the steps, with his eyes fixed on the radiant girl. She stayed behind, ascended to the altar, and, taking the flowers he had laid there, placed them in her bosom.

She stood thus a little while, one hand grasping the crumbling altar-stone, lost in thought.

A large hideous night-owl, which had spent the glaring day in a cool recess, leapt out into the air. Its season of prey-taking had come. The doves, frightened by the rushing of its swooping wings, rose in timid haste and fled away, one one way, the other the other, into the night.

CHAPTER XI.

THE END IS COME OF PLEASANT PLACES.

It was early morning on a day about a month after their visit to Pompeji. The sun had risen behind the Apennines, and was gradually dispelling the thick morning mist that lay over Naples.

There was as yet not much life on the waters of the bay, save where some early fisherman rowed his solitary boat, singing in the clear morning air. It was delightfully cool, and but for the sweet notes of birds among the vines, the eternal splash of the blue waters on the grey rocks, and the far-off *réveillons* of the mighty city, all was silent.

Bianca had risen early, and stood on the terrace looking towards the sea. There was much in harmony between the girl's nature and the moving water. She was restless and always moving.

At this very moment her actions and gestures betrayed her character; for every now and then she would move from her leaning position and pace the terrace, would halt again, and then pace up and down once more.

She was speaking aloud; it was a habit of hers to speak out her thoughts. She had marked the sunrise, and these were her words—

"How like a tyrant the sun is. How blandly, how quietly he rises, hiding carefully the oppression that he harbingers. We hail his approach with joy; it is full of promise, of beauty, gladness, and happiness; but once he is fairly in the heavens, once safely in his throne, once secure from overthrow, he pours forth his darts of fire on those who greeted his birth with acclaim, and whips with scourges of scorpions those who bent before him. And yet I love this emblem. I love the thought of a man thus mastering the world to whom he once did obeisance. . . . *He* said that it was for him to smite the world on the cheek, and I noted how his eyes gleamed when he spoke those words. Oh! he is noble, he is beautiful, he is noble. To dream of such a man all one's youth through and then to find him—is not that enough happiness? To find among a crowd of puppets of men, content with everything simply because things are so satisfied that 'whatever is is right,' inert, without the principle of motion in their flaccid minds, a young man, inspired, angry, discontent, restless, and above all a young man with power and beauty—that is my happiness. I love him, I love him, love, love, love him! To be always with him, to help him in this work, to do battle against that mass of selfish prejudice, to help to tear from the grasping hands of the mob what he claims as his own, to wrench a crown, be it, from the claws of his fellow-men and place it on his head. What would be better than that? I wish he loved me; oh! I do wish he knew that I feel for him, that I would help him to my utmost power, that at his bidding I would leave all that is dear to me, that I would cleave to him all his life, that I would be true to death to him, that I could and would be of great use to him. Why does he not see it? Is he blind? or have I lost that beauty that I had? Are my eyes less bright? Has this burning love wasted me?"

Here she walked from the terrace to the garden, in the centre of which lay a clear, pellucid pool, on which some water-lilies floated.

She bent over it with a questioning look in her flashing eyes. Her hair, loosely fastened with a silver comb, fell in profusion all over her long white neck and shoulders. Holding it back from her eyes with one little white hand she looked at the reflection in the water. Then she knelt down, and plucking a lily turned it round her head, the drops of fresh water gleaming like diamonds between the mottled leaves and the black locks of her hair.

"Is not this enough," she continued, "to attract, to allure? For I want to attract him, and him only."

She tore the lily from her hair with an impatient gesture, and threw it, crushed by her grasp, back into the water.

"I care nothing for this if it is not of his liking. I wish to please him, and him alone. I care not if all Naples, from the king to yonder fisher-lad, call me 'La Bella Bianca.' Bella! Faugh, if not beautiful to him."

With these and other winged words, she returned to her room.

She found Euphrosyne up, and writing at her table. Euphrosyne, too, had been thinking of Charles. But Euphrosyne expressed her thoughts in another way. Whenever anything was strongly and vividly in her thoughts, she wrote.

That is what she had written that morning :—

"Is it not enough to be beautiful, to be noble ? Why does a beautiful and noble being strive for more ? Can worldly greatness enhance these possessions ? Ah ! the sea, the sea, and the handful of sweet flowers withering therein ! To enter the world with a wreath of bays round his head, to have in his hand the lyre of many strings, each thrilling, beneath his touch, to melodious tunes ; to have all the beauties of the world in his eyes, all the warmth of the sun in his heart, all its music in his ears—is not that enough for a man ? To trample his wreath beneath his feet, to prefer the crown of some worldly distinction, to use his sweet-stringed lyre not for love melodies, but for the braying discords of strife, to supplant the innate warmth of his heart with the chill of envy ; to close his eyes to the beauties, his ear to the music of the world of nature, and to race with angry men for some paltry prize. Oh ! why does he do it ? In the stead of an eternal morning, the morning of the awakening child, the fierce blast of noon."

Here Bianca entered, and Euphrosyne, crumpling the paper in her hand, rose to give her greeting.

"So early, loved Bianca?"

"So early, my Euphrosyne!"

"The morning is so beautiful," said Euphrosyne, "that I could not lie abed. There was a little singer in the vines, over there, who seemed to keep bidding me to rise. And then I did not sleep well. I have been thinking."

"Of Arnolfo?" asked Bianca, with a sister's tenderness.

"I have thought much of Arnolfo. I have thought more of him than is good for peace. You know, Bianca mia, that I loved your brother."

"You were a little goose, Euphrosyne," said Bianca, throwing her arms round her friend's neck. "You were a silly little goose. You must not think of Arnolfo. You do not know him. Besides, he is going to be married."

"Married! di Caserta!" said Euphrosyne, opening her blue eyes.

"Yes, married to a lady at Florence. Men will get married, you know."

"Need they?" said Euphrosyne.

"They do, cara, they marry."

"Why?"

"They want a figure head to their table, they want a companion, they want children."

"And, for that, do they marry?"

"Oh! there are other reasons. They love, often at least."

"That word, again," said Euphrosyne; "love, love, and always marriage. Must they go together."

"Few men are content with a Beatrice, or with the memory of a lost Lenore. They want of this world, not of the yonside."

"Do not couple Poe with Dante," said Euphrosyne seriously.

"But tell me, child, you have never told me so before, did you love my brother?"

"I used to think that I should die if he died. I used to think that I lived with him and for him. I used to dream, aye, in day dreams too, of the bliss of being always near him, always with my arms round his neck, like yours are round mine."

"And now?"

"And now I think no more so. I have suffered much, and suffer still to think that all that was a dream. I always knew that Arnolfo did not understand me. Nobody seems to. And now I am glad thereof. Yes, very glad."

"Why?"

"Bianca, I never had a brother, at least I had a brother once. He was a little Garonne-side peasant, I called him Bébé. He was not a real brother, but I thought I felt for him as a sister. Indeed I loved him."

"And?" asked Bianca, after a pause, still holding Euphrosyne in her arms.

"And, well, I know, therefore, what a sister feels. Do you know, I wish I had died when I was a little girl?"

"Euphrosyne!"

"Yes, died. I should have died a child, and rested for ever among the flowers."

"And about Arnolfo?"

"Ah! Arnolfo. Well it is of him that I wish this. I am happy else. I—have—heard—of—Arnolfo—but you are his sister, and I can say no more."

Euphrosyne burst into tears, and Bianca comforted her.

"I know, I know," she said, kissing away the tears, "and that is why I called you a little goose, and said you did not know my brother. I am not very angry with him. Most men are so. At least very many. That is why I am not angry. I should be much happier were it not so; but I was more unhappy for you, for I thought you loved him."

"I did, I did, I did."

"Yes, but loved him as women love men. Loved him so as to become his wife. He is not for you, and you, darling, are not for him. You are a little wild flower from old Garonne, and must be kept from the hot sirocco of the world."

"I am still a child, I know," said Euphrosyne. "I would I were to be a child always. Flowers and music, that is my happiness. You are for the world. You are like a palm-tree, and stand refreshed by the hot blast."

"Yes," cried Bianca, "of the world and against it. Against the hard, cold prejudice, and the withering blast of envy and hate. Refreshed! Yes, and more strong."

Going on to the terrace the two girls heard someone open the gate, and presently Charles appeared, crossing the lawn. He had a tired, dejected air, and walked with hanging head and irresolute step. Now and then he stopped, as if undecided whether to go on. His clothes were disarranged, and his hair in more disorder than ever. He had no hat on, and in one hand he carried a paper.

"Come, there is Carlo," said Bianca; "let us go and meet him, and wish him the good morning."

They descended into the garden. Charles started when he saw Euphrosyne, and drew back.

"You are up early, Signor," said Bianca.

Charles, who looked quite bewildered, said nothing.

"Good morning, Carlo," said Euphrosyne, extending her hand.

Charles seized it, but let it go at once, and said—

"Yes, Signorina, I am early; at least, I have not slept all night."

"A new poem? or a fever! The work, the work!" said Bianca, first laughing, then anxiously.

"Yes, a poem," said Charles with a bitter laugh. "If pain be a poem, most certainly a poem. A poem, if grief and tears be a poem."

"Grief and tears?" said Euphrosyne with an anxious glance at the boy's dejected and weary face.

Charles smiled.

"I am rather dramatic, I fear," said he, "but

there are dramas in our life. I did not expect to see you ladies. I am startled, that is all."

"That is not all," said Bianca impatiently. "Has your work failed?"

"My work has never begun. It was only an angry fancy of mine. Therefore it has not failed since it never existed. No, I thought I should like to see this place again. I love this garden. That is why I came."

Then he took Euphrosyne's hand and kissed it. To Bianca he bowed. Then turning to go, he said—

"I feel like a sleep-walker, and yet I ran all the way here. I stopped an hour at the gate and thought of going back. This seems all strange, does it not? This paper would have explained it, but now that I have seen—you—it is enough. The paper has nothing to explain now."

Charles tore the sheet into pieces, and after standing irresolutely for a minute or two bowed and turned away, turned back, stammered a few words, and finally ran away.

Bianca looked at Euphrosyne; Euphrosyne looked at Bianca.

"The poor boy works too much," said Bianca; "did you see he had no hat on?"

"I only saw his eyes," said Euphrosyne.

"We will ask 'la madre' to invite him to lunch; he will tell us then what is the matter," said Bianca.

The Baroness, who had grown very fond of Charles, readily wrote the invitation, but suggested asking him to dinner instead.

This was agreed upon, and at three o'clock that afternoon the Bienaimée footman took the note round to the Grande Sentinelle.

He returned with this message from the proprietor of the hotel—

"Il Signor Carlo left the hotel this morning, and has gone to Naples. He will not return, he says."

This was the matter. Charles had spent nearly all the remainder of his money in paying his bill the previous evening. He had long foreseen that the moment would come when his funds would be exhausted. New clothes, drives, rows, and other expensive luxuries had soon run away with his money. He had no one to turn for help. Yes, there was Dorothy, but Charles still felt bitter against the little woman. He could not ask her for help. He merely wrote to say, "My funds are quite exhausted, but my courage is not. I leave this place to-morrow, and go to Naples. I can try to live there at any rate. I can drive a cab, row a boat, act as interpreter. That is all."

All the night previous to his departure he had kept awake full of distressful thoughts. That now, of all times, his evil fortune should press upon him was too cruel. He felt that at last Euphrosyne was beginning to like him, he felt that he had some hope, that this strange game he was playing against chance might turn favourably for him; and now by the want of money, by that hard, positive need of money, it seemed as if his last hopes were dashed to the ground.

A leaf from his diary has come into my hands; it expresses fully his feelings on the subject, and I therefore append it—

"At last the day has come when the lotus eater must rise from his bed of voluptuous ease. The north wind has arisen and all the coloured clouds that hid the dark horizon have been rudely blown away. It is finished—that is the sorrow of it.

"Let me calmly review my exact position; let me strip the cold cruel fact of the curtaining robes that my fancy and hopes have woven round it. To-night all the money I have in the world is 465 frcs., this, with a few clothes, some books, and my dear little dog, is all my worldly possession, and I the son of Charles Hauberk. To-morrow I have to pay these people's bill—450 frcs. Remains 15 frcs. I have no one to turn to. John Elphinstone now acknowledges no claim of mine on him, he paid me 6,000 farthings, *et voilá fini.* To Miss Crosthwaite I will not apply—she is not of me, nor for me. She opposes violently the only object I have to live for. I cannot think of her. There is Lovell, the American, but my pride forbids me to ask him. They told me that my proud father would never touch the hand of an inferior. The old gamekeeper from Appledean, whom I met at Oxford, said that often when his work was done the old lord would call him to him and drop a present of gold into his hand, but never touched his hand. And shall I, his son, take from the hand of this man a present, a loan, and shake his hand warmly in gratitude? And what would it avail me if I did? It would postpone my trouble, not destroy it. No, I must go, and beginning at the lowest rung of the ladder battle upwards in the world. My fight will be a harder one; but when the work is over and done the prize will be the sweeter."

And then he had fallen to writing, and the bottom of the leaf of the diary is covered with signatures: Hauberk, Brookshire, and other tokens to show where the poor boy's mind was.

He fell a-thinking then, and Euphrosyne came before his eyes. Gentle, pure Euphrosyne, the little wild flower from old Garonne side. He had learnt to know her better the last few days, and this knowledge had fed his love. Charles was not of a vulgar mind, he had himself quite under control, and shunned vice, not only because its hideousness was abhorrent to him, but because he felt a pride in himself which forbade his stooping to join in the low and vulgar pleasures of other young men.

At the University he was noted for his rigorous observance of this inborn principle of his. "It is not gentlemanly," he used to say, when any blue story was started at his "wines," and few of the undergraduates who were present that May morning, at Lord H—'s breakfast party at the "House," will forget how Charles Hauberk Benson walked out of my lord's room, when my lord, warmed with the strong posset, began to entertain his guests with anecdotal heirlooms, handed down to my lord by his worthy three-bottle ancestors.

"It is not gentlemanly," he said, bowing to my lord. "You did not invite me here, I know, to offend me, and I will go before I begin to regret accepting your hospitality."

With this unbending repugnance to vice in men Charles was infinitely stricter in his ideas about women. The word "woman" was in his mind a word full of infinite suggestion of praise, and he classed as among a third sex, a sex of pariahs, all the filthy of men and women, even those whom the world passed as models of all that is good, but who hide behind the fig-leaves of the world's opinion all uncleanness. A woman to Charles was a being pure as a marble statue; an evil thought, a loose word, a veiled suggestion, even the merest breath of the winds that fan Priapus, in a woman, rendered her no longer a woman in his opinion.

He had found in the world few "women," very, very few; but at last he had found Euphrosyne. Yes, Euphrosyne, and that was the end of all. Here was a woman. He loved her; why seek for more? And now he was to lose her, and be banished from her fair presence to the lowest grades of poverty, and unromantic poverty, of hard, dirty, vulgar, vicious poverty.

The sun had dawned upon him still thinking. It woke him from his dreams and brought into light all the misery of the fact. He started to his feet. He could see Euphrosyne once more, or at least the home of Euphrosyne. He wrote a few lines on a paper.

"I leave this for a good-bye. I may never see you again. Still I love you. Do you find that strange? It is so, and the misery is that I must go. Addio, Euphrosyne, addio."

Then he had run out of his room just as he was, and to the Villa Dresda. At the gates he had waited an hour. At last he entered. His interview with Euphrosyne has been described.

That day he left, Herbert had gone on an excursion to Amalfi, and so he had no explanations to make. He left most of his things with the proprietor. Fang accompanied him. He reached Naples almost penniless. He took with him a small drawing, very precious to him now. It represented a handful of flowers cast loose on an angry sea.

CHAPTER XII.

QUAE MEDICAMENTA NON SANANT, FERRUM SANAT.

POVERTY, grim, dirty, itching, poverty; this is what stared the *soi-disant* heir of all the Hauberks in the face, and now at last was he to be tried. His trials heretofore had been trials of temper, but now the bitterer trials of want, real, hard want were to prove of what metal he was made.

Whatever may have been his innermost thoughts on the subject, he certainly revealed no great emotion as he stepped from the steamer into the little boat that was to land him at Naples. Dressed in a pale, green-tinted cashmere suit, the jacket carelessly buttoned over a striped blue and white shirt, with a red and blue silk cap on his black hair, and a silk scarf of the St. Mary's colours twisted into a negligent sailor's knot round his neck, he looked rather like a leisurely young Englishman, taking his pleasure in a peculiar fashion, than like a man whose last resources were exhausted, who knew not how his next meal would be got, or where he would lay his head that night.

"Come, Fang," said Charles, jumping lightly on to the landing, after giving the barcaiuolo eight times his fare, in his Hauberky, *noblesse oblige* faculty.

Charles was never happy but when he had a

cigarette between his teeth, and as he found his case empty, he strolled up to the Debito in the Toledo, where the Laferme better qualities are sold, and bought a box at five francs.

With these and a *Daily News* (price one franc), and a lemon granita, he passed a pleasant hour in front of the Café de l'Europe. At about six o'clock, seeing the carriages go by, Chiaja-wards, he thought he would take a drive. Two hours afterwards he was set down again in the Piazza del Plebiscito with exactly eight sous in his pocket, feeling very hungry. Fang was taking his evening meal off a bone he had found. Charles eyeing him said—

"Go shares, Fang." But Fang turned a deaf ear to his proposal, and Charles remained hungry.

He had not enough money to order a *consommation* at the *café*, and could not thus enter, and so went and sat down on the steps of the Royal Chapel to await his destiny.

Meanwhile Charles began to experience sensations which he had never felt before. Cold and hunger. We often talk of being "fearfully cold," or "awfully hungry," but the immediate prospect of allaying our suffering deadens it very much. When there is no such prospect, then, indeed, is cold fearful, and hunger awful. But still he sat on, trying to string together some rhymes on Euphrosyne.

Night came on, and for very cold he was obliged to rise and walk about. Whither? No hotel would take him in without baggage, he could not go into a restaurant and act Mungo, and he was sufficiently worldly to know that English Consuls and other representatives of Her Britannic Majesty are never "prepared to enter into your case to-night, but will take it into consideration, the fee being," &c., and that foreign chaplains want to know when last you attended Holy Communion at their chapel before helping you.

"I will walk about all night," said Charles.

It began to rain. He turned up his collar, and lit a cigarette. The rain put it out. As he turned, very hungry now, into the Strada del Molo, an old hag came up, and with the usual preface of "Muori di fam," entreated his help. He went on. She followed him.

"Oh, beautiful gentleman, Oh, rich milor, help poor Maria, for the love of your Excellency's patron saint."

"Poor Maria," said Charles, smiling, "will you change purses with me?"

But poor Maria did not understand, and continued her doleful plaint. She really seemed in great distress.

Charles plunged his hand into his pocket and gave her five sous, saying—

"Poor Maria! you are now richer than I."

Behind the Molo, or pier of Naples, lie some of the poorest houses of that impoverished town. It is here that the *lazzaroni* lie out the night, and it is here that all the *rodeurs* of the quays congregate.

In this quarter Charles had now come. It was

ten o'clock at night, and he had tasted nothing all day but his first slight breakfast and a lemon sorbetto. He was, in all truth, "awfully" hungry. He happened to pass a wretched hovel, on the window of which was traced in red letters, *Trattoria della Marina.* He stopped and looked at it. The door opened and a beggar lad was flung out into the street with a *Va Birbo!* At the same time an odour of hot maccaroni filled Charles's nostrils, and, loathsome as the place looked, he could not resist any longer and entered.

The room was a dirty, dark place, with a range at the further end, where a large cauldron full of maccaroni was cooking. A few filthy tables formed all the accommodation for the guests of the *Trattoria della Marina.*

The place was crowded with beggars eating their sou's worth of the farinaceous delight out of wooden basins, which were chained to the wall. Some used their hands to convey their food to their mouths, others, in true Neapolitan style, had left their basins on the table, and plunging their faces into the contents, seized a portion of the stringy food with their teeth, threw their heads back and swallowed it.

The padrone came up to Charles, who ordered three sous' maccaroni. The man then went to the cauldron, fished out three handfuls with his hands, brought them in a basin to Charles, who had taken his place at one of the tables, poured it into a basin which a beggar had just used, and wished Charles "*Buon' appetito.*"

Charles was going to begin, when the proprietor placed his dirty hand on the food, saying, "You pay in advance." Charles felt in his pocket and turned hot and cold. He had only two sous left. He told the padrone.

"*Fa niente,*" said he, and took a handful of the maccaroni out of the basin which he retransferred to the cauldron.

Charles shut his eyes and began to eat, and so hungry was he that he finished the whole of his portion, and enjoyed it too!

Having finished his repast, Charles went out into the street again, feeling a greasier, yet a happier man. It had cleared up, and the moon shone down clear on the muddy, garbage-covered streets. Truly old Naples presents a wonderful sight, and in few other places, I think, does one meet with such narrow streets, bounded by houses which count twelve, thirteen, and fourteen stories.

It was while walking about here that Charles began really to recognise the depths of poverty. The cabaret he had just left was poverty in all conscience, but it represented Poverty having *something.* What he saw here showed him that even amongst the poorest there are great lines and degrees, that a man possessed of three-farthings is relatively better off than the man who has nothing, than a king is better off than the possessor of the three-farthings. Here he saw Poverty having *nothing! nothing! nothing!*

There lay a woman lying half in the gutter, her head pillowed on the damp kerbstone, while large rats chased each other over her muddy form, or fought, squealing, for the possession of a mildewed cabbage leaf, that had been blown from a heap of garbage on to her mud-stained breast. Here sat a man, dressed only so as to make his nakedness more visible, filling his empty body by munching a piece of melon rind. Huddled up in another corner lay three boys, two of whom were absolutely naked, the third had put his little legs into the arms of an old coat. Across the road lay a dead man; further on a dead cat, while a strangled dog to the right completed the trio. The rats were busy about all three, but gave the man the preference. The pavement was literally one mass of filth, mud, vegetables, blood, animal refuse, all pounded together, and steaming with the rain that had lately fallen. Save for a little oil lamp at the corner of the street, burning before an image of the Madonna, who, apparently consoled by the motto carved on the stone beneath—

HE HATH FILLED THE HUNGRY WITH GOOD THINGS,

was beaming over the foul sight, the moon was the only light that lit this mournful scene. Charles, sickened, left it. Fang, in his element among the rats, was prone to stay.

"Where am I to sleep to-night?" said Charles, two hours later, as he sat on a bench outside the Villa del Popolo, watching the ox-drawn carts, heavily laden with all kinds of market produce, labour along the roads into the centre of the town. Somebody, passing behind him at the moment, stopped. Charles was too sleepy to notice him. The man went on again.

"How cold and wretched it is, is it not, Fang? but I fear we must make a night of it here on this stone bench," continued Charles, rising to stretch his limbs, aching with fatigue and cold. As he stood up, he saw opposite to him, a coloured lamp on which was written—

"Qui si dorma."

"Any shelter in a storm," thought Charles, making for the door; then he stopped, and sorrowfully returned to his seat. He remembered. He had not even the price of a bed in yonder refuge.

"Qui si dorma," continued he, stretching himself out on the bench, "unless a gend'arme comes up."

As he was laying himself out on the bench the jingling of some coins roused him. He jumped up, and saw a few coins lying on the pavement. Fivepence in all.

Without stopping to think whence they came, or whom they belonged to, but registering a mental I O U to the profit of their former owner, Charles took them, walked across the street and entered the refuge.

"Can I sleep here?" he asked of a woman who met him on the stairs.

"Si, Signor, there's room in number 5."

"Can my dog come in?"

"No."

"Then I can't."

"Stay, if you pay for the dog you may bring him."

"How much a bed?"

"A franc each."

"I will give you twopence."

"Agreed."

The woman led him to a long, low room, where about thirty men and boys were lying asleep on a row of mattresses, covered with filthy blankets. They were all huddled together for warmth, but the woman found Charles a place. Fang was relegated to a corner. The woman bade Charles stroke himself down before lying down. She gave this order to every customer. For Neapolitans she was perhaps right. Charles did not take her meaning. He lay down, feeling too tired to be ashamed, and was soon fast asleep.

It would take too long to tell how Charles fared during the rest of the week; suffice it to say that by pawning his watch and a few other gold trinkets which he had about him, he managed to live. During this time he was not inactive, and firmly resolved not to pester his few friends for help, he set about to try to find employment. This was almost impossible.

He at first thought of giving English lessons, and indeed went to a registry office for that purpose. He was, however, discouraged by the proprietor, who said, "At Naples we eat and drink, and don't learn English. We are too lazy."

He would not go as a domestic servant, he preferred to starve. At last he found work, curious employment, forsooth, for an Oxford undergraduate, to row a boat for hire, but this was what Charles did, and he did it well too, his Oxford training helping him in the rowing, and creating much envy among the other barcaiuoli. By this employment he earned about seven francs a day, enough to keep himself and Fang. He rented a small room in the Strada Medina for twenty francs a month, and ate his meals *al fresco*, thus, perforce, tasting the poverty to which he had previously resolved himself. I do not know if he was happy all this time, but he looked remarkably well, and the exercise and fresh air freshened his face up and made him handsomer than ever; indeed, he looked so well, and made such a picturesque appearance in his quaint costume, that he got more custom than many of his colleagues. His pride—well, he had swallowed that; and though he felt the Hauberk tradition as strongly as ever, deadened all peevish remonstrances that he sometimes made to himself.

One day, business being very slack, he was standing in the glorious sunshine warming himself and smoking, leaning against the custom-house, when he heard himself addressed in Italian.

"I have found you—come."

He looked up; it was a stranger who had addressed him. The stranger was rather tall, and dressed in the negligent way which artists sometimes affect. He had very dark flowing hair, large rolling eyes, and rather an oriental type of feature, and a most intelligent and interesting expression. He wore spectacles, which seemed to burn with the fire that flashed from his magnificent eyes.

"I have found you," he repeated; "come."

"Whither?" answered Charles in Italian. "Does the gentleman want a row?"

"No," answered the stranger in English, "not a row, my friend. I want you. Come," he continued, "I will speak to you, but not here. Let us go into that *café*. There, what will you take?"

"Your meaning," said Charles.

"You shall have that," said the artist, "but what else?"

"Listen," continued he, when he and Charles had been served with a cool drink each, "I want to tell you something. Will you sit as a model to me?"

Charles rose and said indignantly—

"Yes, because you see me among a herd of swine you take me for one too; because you see my hands rough and hardened you take me for a common fellow, who wishes to pick up money as best he can. I have to work to live, but the work you offer is an insult to me. I am Charles Hauberk."

"You will not refuse me," said the artist gently. "I meant no insult. Were you the archangel Gabriel himself I should ask you. Do you know that I have a picture to paint, a picture that is to excel every picture yet painted, a picture that shall be hereafter a landmark in a barren wilderness, and shall rise from out the desert of to-day's art like a pyramid amid the sands. I have to redeem the nineteenth century."

"You have a great work to do," said Charles bitterly.

"Yes, but I will do or I will die. I will be with Raffael and Boticelli or I will be not at all; and I have in my head what, if worked out, will give a place near his side, near Raffael's side. This is what I want you to help me to do."

"A thorough man of the world," said Charles, "might find your proposal not quite disinterested."

"With the world of to-day," answered the artist, "I have nothing to do. I feel as if I was not of it, or in it. I want to do this work, and then I do not care what comes of me. Listen: I have to paint the Archangel Gabriel himself. The idea came to me one day as I walked the plain of Marathon alone. I do not know why the inspiration came to me there; perhaps that standing where my ancestors did such noble deeds I felt inspired to do likewise and my victory, for I will conquer, will be as great as theirs. Single-handed I will put the barbarians to flight, these beer-jug, race-day artists of to-day, who call themselves sons of art, but whose works are mere smears on wasted canvas, whose art, be it, never rises above photography, indeed never rises so far, and who personify vulgarity for the vulgar. These genre-painters, let them paint signboards for their living; I will paint archangels, or I will die. Now, vivid as my impression of the mighty angel is I must have a model, and to find one who would in any way be suitable I have traversed nearly the whole earth. I have ransacked the quarters where models congregate in London, Paris, Rome, Berlin, in fact everywhere; I have sought my prototype amongst the peasants of the Ionian and the Shetland Islands, in Zealand and Corfu, in Brazil and Putney, but I have never found what I sought till I found you. Fellow-worker, will you help me?"

"You flatter me in offering me a share in so certain a victory. I fear I have little of the angel in me."

"Come."

And holding him tight Kallandros the artist led Charles to a carriage, and they drove away.

At the studio, Kallandros bade Charles strip and pose, and set to work in all haste to fill in the outlines of his sketch.

"Have you any sorrow? Have you anything to make you indignant? Have you any enemy?" asked Kallandros after a while.

Then Charles's rage burst out—

"Enemy!" he cried. "The world. My enemy, the whole, whole world, the bearded men, the smooth-faced women. I hate them all. They lie of me; they insult me daily."

"Yes, yes," said Kallandros in the greatest trepidation lest Charles should forget his anger, for the fierce expression of his face and his dilating eyes produced the very effect that Kallandros wanted. "The world is insolent, I know."

"Insolent!" said Charles, "it is a mass of insolence! The son of nobody. Grocers, drapers, sink-lifters, all say that of me. Filius nullius. Nobody's son, or the son of the mob. The offspring of the *canaille.*"

"Ah, the *canaille*," said Kallandros, working with all his might, "they claim you as their son do they? Here, take this sword and hold it thus."

"Yes, see me here an artist's model, see me there rowing paunchy bourgeois at two soldi a head, see me there squabbling with tipsy fishwives or English tourists for my wage, and then say if my life is not one of perpetual insult."

"You are a gentleman by birth, of course?"

"No, I tell you, I am nobody's son. I am no gentleman."

"There," said Kallandros, "I have finished; it is enough."

"Now offer me money," said Charles, "and complete it."

"My poor fellow," said the artist kindly, "whatever your suffering may be, and your indignation can arise from no small suffering, do not mind. If you despise the world, rise above it. Rise from dirty materialism to art. You may be an artist, and not know how to draw a line; you may be a poet, and never have rhymed one word to another. But for this perception of the beautiful all men are equal, from emperors down to the filthy crowd where first I saw you. Leave them and join the bright choirs of beautiful souls, and happiness will come to you. Here," continued he, drawing a beautiful sapphire ring from his finger, "take this as a souvenir of me."

"I can offer you no souvenir in exchange," said Charles.

"This is my souvenir of you," said Kallandros, pointing to the canvas.

At this moment the servant entered and said that two gentlemen wished to see Mr. Kallandros.

"Who are they?" asked the artist.

"I do not know," said the servant." "Two well-dressed gentlemen. They particularly wish to see you."

"Let them enter," said Kallandros.

Charles, who had not finished dressing, deprecated, but it was too late. Kallandros had forgotten that it was no ordinary model he had with him.

The door opened and there entered—

The Chevalier de la Vigne and Mr. Mangles!

With a cry of shame Charles gathered his clothes about him, dashed the sapphire ring on the ground, and fled from the room.

It was too late, and as he was rushing down the passage, he heard Mangles say in his vulgar English—

"Well, here's a jolly come-down; Benson an artist's model, eh?"

To which the Chevalier added—

"And he has had the presumption to shake hands with Alphonse de le Vigne, and to sit at the same table as Placide, Baroness de Bienaimée. *La canaille!*"

CHAPTER XIII.

QUAE FERRUM NON SANAT, IGNIS SANAT.

"What medicines cannot cure, iron cures; what iron cannot cure, fire cures." So said Hippocrates. It is by our failings that we suffer most, for, as these always prove stumbling-blocks to us in our path of life, we learn that our sufferings come most often from them. Sometimes, but rarely, we are sufficiently wise to draw benefit from the hard knocks they cause us to receive; oftener we only tighten our lips, shrug our shoulders, and from very obstinacy continue to foster what we know will bring us pain and punishment. Medicines, hot irons, and fire are all successively applied by the world to cure us, and nearly always fail, for corporal and mental maladies have little in common beyond producing pain. Each application either cures us or intensifies our malady.

How was it with Charles? Surely his pride had been attacked so severely as to make him wish to abandon it. Look at the graduated tumbles it had received—his leaving Oxford with the attending circumstances, the different rebuffs he had received from the commonest of people, the suspicion he had been met with everywhere, the final, total collapse he had suffered in purse, his night amongst the poorest of the poor, sleeping in one bed with the outcasts and offscourings of society, his forced menial employment, and finally his being found posing for an artist by these two men, whom he had always treated as positive inferiors.

As he himself said, as he got back into the street—

"What further humiliations can there be for me? I have drunk the cup to its dregs."

And then he sorrowfully fell a-thinking of his life, of what he might have made of his past, of his dreadful present, and of the future which presented no hope, and at last he saw how much of wilfulness and folly he had to reproach himself with.

"I have brought all this on myself," he cried bitterly, sinking on to a seat by the roadside, and burying his face in his hands. "I have broken my life."

What was he to do? The life he had led so far during the last week could surely not last. He could not bring himself to the prospect of always rowing for a livelihood; he, with his brain teeming with vitality and straining always after fuller, ampler knowledge, to live always a machine! And yet there seemed nothing else for him to do. He, who had hoped some day to overcome all obstacles, and place on his head again the coronet which he claimed as his own, to earn his livelihood always by rowing a boat. The option was starvation. Now that the novelty and the romance of his position had worn off, how very sorry it seemed. And then, strong and lithe as he was, he was not strong enough to bear continually the hot noonday sun, and the endless, severe toil, that the clumsy, heavy boat inflicted on him. He had swallowed his pride, yes, indeed he had, and had for the time being cheerfully done the work that had come to his hand, with a strength and courage that surprised even himself.

For what young English gentleman, blue-blooded and refined, would, taken from a comfortable and refined life, from an obsequious crowd of servants, from the society of intelligent men and refined women, be able to buckle themselves down to the coarse, hard, undignified life of a common ferryman, and know how to take the copper coins they earned with grace. Charles had done this, but he felt he could do it no more. But what was he to do? Charles lighted a cigarette.

Just then somebody ran up to him, crying—

"My dear fellow, I've found you at last."

It was Herbert Lovell.

Charles was not very pleased, but he took Herbert's hand.

"Why, Hauberk," continued he, "what have you been doing? Money bothers, eh? Well, you know, you ought to have come to me about that, and not go away like you did."

"I have not yet said that I left the Grande Sentinelle Hotel for financial reasons," answered Charles.

"Financial reasons?" said Herbert, laughing. "What stiff terms."

"I feel anything but stiff," said Charles, regaining his good humour under the genial influence of the American's laugh. "Quite the contrary."

"Well," said the American, "where are you staying?"

"Strada Medina, No. 9, 8th story, on the back."

"What are you doing?"

"Talking to you."

"No, but what do you do all day?"

"Row a boat."

"Row a boat, all day? In this heat?"

"I don't row for pleasure, I live by it."

"Nonsense."

"Nonsense or not here is my licence, and here is my number as barcaiuolo, and here is my tariff."

"But you surely don't mean to say you are forced to do this?"

"I am *forced* to do nothing, I prefer it to blacking boots."

"Have you no money?"

"Yes, five francs; I earned them this morning."

"But that is all nonsense, and can't go on. Come back with me to Sorrento, and be my guest."

"Your guest, for the rest of my natural life?"

"If you like."

"Thank you, you are very kind. I prefer to row a boat."

"Thanks."

"I mean I could not think of accepting your offer; I am obliged to work, and do not mind it. It is only temporary."

"Then if only temporary, come and tide your difficulties over with me."

"No, Lovell, don't press me. I am suffering now the effects of a very great folly, and enjoy my punishment. I feel it does me good. Do not tempt me."

"But, my dear fellow, how can I see a friend, and a friend like you, in such a position?"

"Do I look so very miserable?"

"No; on the contrary, you look remarkably well. Quite the type of the handsome boatman."

"I was taken for the archangel Gabriel just now."

"And look it. But do listen to reason."

"I do; I listen to my own reason, and I prefer to work to increasing my obligations to you. If you want to befriend me recommend your friends to patronize my boat."

Herbert renewed his invitation, but Charles was firm. At last Herbert asked him to accompany him to the post-office.

Charles answered—

"You will be ashamed to be seen with me."

Herbert took his arm in answer.

As they were walking up the street to the post-office Herbert told Charles that they had a new *pensionnaire* at the hotel.

"Whom?" asked Charles.

"A very objectionable young man."

"What is his name?"

"Mangles."

"Oh, oh, I knew him at Oxford. A brewer's

son, a very unpleasant fellow; very low and common."

"Both. He knows you. He has made a lot of evil talk about you."

"Indeed. I owe him money. Hinc illae lacrimae."

The post-office was now reached, and Herbert went to get his letters. Charles waited for him in the yard.

Standing thus, the thought came that there might be something for him. So he went to the H counter and asked for letters for Hauberk. There were three, and one which the official would not give up unless he produced his passport.

"I have none," said Charles.

"Then," said the official, "the letter must be brought to your lodging. Where do you live?"

"Strada Medina, No. 9, 8th floor."

The first letter bore the superscription office, "Telegram, Poste Restante." The stamp on the envelope was several days old.

Charles tore it open. It was a telegram from Keswick, from Miss Crosthwaite—

"*Charles Hauberk, Post Restante, Naples. Dear Chas. Received most important communication from John Elphinstone. Am writing to-night.*
"*Dorothy Crosthwaite.*"

What could this be? With beating heart and trembling hand he tore open the second packet, a letter from Dorothy.

Dorothy's letter was short.

"DEAREST CHARLES,

"Things are coming right. Elphinstone has got back some of your funds, and has acted honestly. Read his letter. I wish you all success and happiness, only don't like addressing to Poste Restantes.

"Your affectionate,

"DOROTHY."

"P.S.—Don't forget Spider Harrison and others."

The third letter was from John Elphinstone, addressed to Charles at Keswick, and forwarded by Dorothy.

"MY DEAREST CHARLES,

"I have much pleasure in writing to tell you that I can now in some measure redeem my promise of restitution, made to you when I was bound to confess that I had wasted all the money left with me in trust for you.

Some of the investments which I made in your name, and which at the period of my bankruptcy seemed only so much waste paper, have been looking up lately in a remarkable manner, and are paying good dividends. At that time they were absolutely worthless, besides being taken in your name, they escaped the trustees of my creditors.

"I have managed to save about £3,000, and the interest of this, from the time since I stopped paying your allowance, I forward to you through Miss Crosthwaite. The sum of £3,000 is at your disposal, and on hearing from you I will either forward you the papers, or sell out and pay the money into any bank you please.

"I shall be glad to hear from you what arrangements you propose.

"Charlotte and the children are well, and send love.

"Believe me, with sincerest congratulations, my dear Charles,

"Your affectionate Guardian,

"JOHN LUKE ELPHINSTONE.

"Devizes."

"What is the matter with you?" said Herbert, who had finished his business, and seeing Charles reel against one of the courtyard pillars, pale and breathless, had hurried to his friend's side. "What is the matter? No bad news?"

Charles as a pauper, and Charles with an income, were two different men.

"No," said Charles, "the heat rather overcame me, but excuse me, Mr. Lovell, I must go to my apartment. I have some business to do."

"But where shall we meet, Hauberk? You know I positively refuse to allow my friend to continue in the state I found you in. You must come back to the hotel with me until things are settled."

"My dear Mr. Lovell, do not disturb yourself on my account. I have odd whims at times, but do not, when they are foolish, care to be reminded about them. I pulled a boat out of romantic folly. Please do not remind me of it, and please do not repeat an offer I have already declined with thanks. I shall probably return to the Grande Sentinelle, or perhaps, as the society there is not of the best, put up at the Victoria or Tramontano Hôtel."

"Well," said Lovell, "I can't tell you how glad I am, but, dear Charles, don't indulge in whims of that sort again. You cannot imagine how distressed I was to hear you had left so suddenly, and under such circumstances. I did my best to find you, and have not had a day's quiet till I found you, but have been running up and down Naples asking everywhere for you. Do promise me not to do so again. For you know, Charles," said he, with tenderness, "we are to be good friends."

"Yes," said Charles, "but do not let us rehearse Orestes and Pylades here. People are looking. I am extremely obliged to you for your kind expressions of sympathy towards myself, but, as I stated, I have business to attend to. *Au revoir.*"

And he walked away hastily. Herbert stood still looking sadly after him. Then turning slowly away, he said, in a half-whisper, "And I love him as a brother."

Charles got to the door of the house where he lived, feeling very excited and happy at the wonderful and sudden change in his fortunes, and yet imbued with that essentially human feeling of irritation that comes to all people whose unjust sufferings have been removed, that this relief came late and did not at all compensate for the pain he had endured. But deeper still lay another feeling that had grown stronger and stronger as he had walked away from Herbert. Struggling with this, he stood in silence outside the door of the house for a few moments, then suddenly he tightened his belt, and ran at full speed back to the post-office.

Herbert was no longer there, and, after searching for him in vain, Charles went to the telegraph office, and wrote hastily the following short telegram:—

"*Dear Herbert I am a d—d cad. Forgive me.*
"CHARLES"

Having done this, he walked slowly back again, proud, erect as ever. When he got home he went upstairs to his room and lay down, and closing his eyes tried to realise that all his sufferings were now at an end, and that although still poor he had a competence, and need never again be exposed to the insults of a class which he despised. His head was very hot, and the blood tingled in his hands, and he felt like a man who had suffered a severe blow; but all this almost painful excitement was, *au fond*, a pleasant sensation.

He was not to be spared another trial, however. A knock came to his door, and then entered the master of the floor he lived on.

"Sir," said he, "pay me."

"Certainly," said Charles, rising. The possessor of £3,000 would do that.

"Pay me my money."

"How much?"

"A week's rent, five francs."

Charles put his hand into his pocket as if to find his £3,000 there. It was empty. He had paid away his last sou in telegraphing to Herbert.

"Wait a little," said he.

"No I won't," blustered the man. "If you can't pay five francs you're no good. I knew you had no money. You row a boat. I don't let my room to Camorristi!"

"You must wait," said Charles, "I am expecting money to-day.

"Aye, aye, from the Queen of Italy, eh? Who owes you money? *Carogna!* You lie a-bed and cheat honest folks. *Birbone f—*"

"I tell you you must wait," said Charles, quietly.

"And I tell you I won't, *barcaioul!* Pay me now. You have nothing. I will take your dog. He will make soup. Dog and *figlio d' un cane;* pay me."

"I cannot."

"I will take your dog."

"You will not."

"I will."

"You are an insolent scoundrel," said Charles, bursting into a torrent of wrath. "A disgraceful, insolent ruffian."

The man stepped up to him, he was a tall, powerful fellow, struck him down, and kicked him on the head. Charles lay stunned, but Fang, hurling himself at the man, revenged his master, and the cowardly Italian ran, shrieking to the Madonna for help, bleeding from the dog's savage bites, out of the room.

Whom medicines cure not, iron cures, whom iron cures not, fire cures. It was indeed consummated. Their lay beaten on to the ground by a gutter-born keeper of lodgings, Charles Hauberk, *soi-disant* eighth earl of Brookshire, helpless, penniless, and insulted with the greatest insult. Pride trodden to the very ground by Dirt and Insolence. The beggar had beaten the aristocrat. The Italian thief had lain the English gentleman low.

From his sleep of unconsciousness, Charles was roused by a series of growls and snappy barks, and becoming conscious, found himself lying on the floor. Fang lay by his side with his paws on his master's chest, and was growling viciously at a man who had entered the room.

"Call your dog off," said the stranger, "or I will go away."

"Who's there? What is it? Fang, lie down. Where am I?"

"Here, you've got to sign this," said the man, a postman, holding out a receipt book and a registered letter. "Sharp, too, or I'll go away."

Charles signed mechanically, and took the letter, then feeling giddy, he walked to his bed and lay down.

"Have you nothing for the postman? I've come up eight stories," said the man viciously.

"No, come to-morrow, I have no change."

With a "*maledetto birbo*" the man went away.

As soon as Charles had recovered a little he opened his letter. It contained a line from Dorothy, and a cheque on Turnbull & Co. for £270, forwarded through Miss Crosthwaite by John Elphinstone.

CHAPTER XIV.

THE CHEVALIER PROPOSES.

"Euphrosyne."

"Yes, little mother."

"Come here, my child, I have to talk seriously with you."

Euphrosyne looked as grave as possible, and going up to her mother, seated herself on a little footstool at her feet.

"What is it, little mother?"

The Baroness threw one arm round the girl's fair neck, and smoothing the profusion of brown hair off her daughter's forehead, began the serious talk.

"Dear child—or rather dear daughter, for it is not to the child I speak, but to my grown-up young lady—you are now old enough to understand what I have to say to you. You will marry some day"—

"Marry, mamma? Why marry?"

"It is every woman's duty, and certainly the duty of intelligent and beautiful women, to share their joys and sorrows with a man. You will marry some day; you are even now being sought in marriage."

"No, mamma."

"Have you never received pressing attentions from any of the gentlemen who come here—the Chevalier—"

A merry laugh interrupted her. Then with eyes wide open and a pretty little blush, Euphrosyne said—

"No, no, mamma, never. You don't think he wants me, do you mamma?"

"Yes, child, he came to Naples on purpose."

"How very silly of him! Oh, mamma, how could you think of him. I mustn't marry *him*, must I?"

"There is no *must* in the matter. You shall marry whom you please. I will never constrain you, and though my only purpose in life is now to see you happy, I would rather see you condemned to the chill of eternal spinsterhood than marry you to anyone against your wish. But what I want to say to you is not this."

The Baroness opened a writing case that lay on the table, and took from it a sealed packet, on which was written in faded ink—

"*To be read to my darling daughter, Euphrosyne, on her eighteenth birthday.*"

Euphrosyne caught at the letter, and then with her eyes filling with tears, said in a low voice—

"It is poor papa."

"Yes, child," answered the Baroness very gravely, and repressing a sigh, "it is from your father. He wrote this on the eve of the fatal day, when he died in defence of his honour, and gave it to me, bidding me follow the direction, should anything happen to him. I have told you the rest," said the Baroness breaking down.

"Yes," said Euphrosyne, rising to her feet, and

kissing away the tears that had welled up in her mother's eyes. "Yes I am proud of papa. *Notre honneur avant notre vie*, is our motto, and he died for that."

After a little while the Baroness proceeded—"To-day is your eighteenth birthday, and to-day I will break this seal and read your father's dying words, his last command to you."

"Stay, mother, tell me. Did papa love me very much?"

"Yes, my child."

"What did he say to me as I lay in my cradle that night? Tell me again."

"He bent over you, and kissed you, and kissed you, and took your little hand in his and said—

"'Little daughter, be a true daughter of your father, be a true Bienaimée.'"

"And am I?"

The Baroness kissed her daughter in reply; then she opened the packet and read—

"My Daughter,

"The last words of your father are—

"'*Marry a gentleman, a man of honour, and be worthy of him.*'

"My blessing and eternal love be upon you and with you always.

"Your Father,

"Gilleroy

de Bienaimée."

The Baroness then kissed the signature, and folding the letter up again, gave it to her daughter.

"When he gave me that packet years ago," she continued, "he said that he had but one thing to tell you, for the rest he trusted to me."

"Poor little father," said Euphrosyne tenderly.

"Well, now you know his wish. You are to marry a gentleman."

"What do *you* call a gentleman, mamma?"

"A man of good family, of untarnished name, of legitimate birth, who has a full respect in all cases for the feelings of others, who lives within his income, and does not endeavour to increase it by acts unbecoming his position or his honour," said the Baroness rather pointedly.

"Is Arnolfo a gentleman?" said Euphrosyne, with a tinge of sorrow in her tone.

"Certainly, certainly, my child," said the Baroness, quickly, "most certainly."

"Who does not endeavour to increase his income by acts unbecoming his position," said Euphrosyne, quoting her mother's words. "Is gambling unbecoming?"

"N—o," answered Mme. de Bienaimée. "I think not. All gentlemen gamble; your father did. It is a bad habit, but it has caste."

"Well, is de la Vigne a gentleman?"

"Yes, my child, he is. And talking about Alphonse, I want to tell you what I suspect you know, that he wants to marry you."

"Why do you say so?"

"His uncle, a relation of mine, wrote to me, asking me if I did not think that a marriage between you two would be a very good thing."

"Mother," said Euphrosyne gravely, "please tell your relation, de la Vigne's uncle, that it would be a bad thing, a very bad thing."

"My child?"

"Yes, mother, you cannot know me if you think such a thing possible. I do not know much about men and women, and the ways of the world, but what I do know, and what I feel as vividly as I feel my heart beat, is that de la Vigne is no gentleman."

"Euphrosyne!"

"I have an instinctive horror of the man. A little while ago, I was quite a child then, I felt I wanted to laugh at him, now I feel inclined to run away when I see him."

"Dearest?"

"Yes, run away. I think I know him well enough. I am to marry a gentleman, you know."

"Well, child, I said I would in no way constrain you; and though de la Vigne is very elegant, dresses well, and has an independent income, I must say I should like you to become the wife of a manlier man."

"Is Charles Hauberk a gentleman?"

"*No*," cried the Baroness, almost angrily.

"Mother?"

"No, no, no. In no single point. He is of no family, of less than no family. He is here under a false name. He has no money, no income"—

"How do you know all this?" said Euphrosyne.

"I have it from a former friend, a creditor, by the way, of his, that Mr. Man-geles, who has been staying here, who was presented by Alphonse. His real name is Benson; he ran away from England because he could not stay there any longer, because he had made dishonest debts. He lives as best he can, by adventuring. He rows boats, he is an artist's model, he does anything to live."

"I am sorry for that," said Euphrosyne, winding her mother's arm off her neck, and rising to her feet. "I am very sorry for that, for"—

"For"—

"I love Charles Hauberk, and if I am to leave you for any man it will be to be with him always. I love him."

"But Euphrosyne, this is very wrong. I tell you what this young man is. Remember your father's last words."

"To marry a gentleman. He is one."

"But, child, I have already told you he is not. You have heard what I have said."

"I love him."

"You may love him or not, you have no right to do so. I forbid it—your dead father forbids it."

"I think Carlo a gentleman."

"But he is not. He has a false name; he does wrong things—he does common things."

"For me he has no other name but—The Beautiful. In my eyes he does nothing but sing sweet songs."

"He rows a ferryboat one day, he lives in a princely villa the next, next day he strips and poses to an artist for hire."

"Because one day he has no money, the next he has no strength."

"Euphrosyne, do not argue with me. You must not think of him."

"I think of him only."

"But it is wrong, very wrong; he is not of your class, of your kind; he is of low birth."

"The rose-tree rises from the ground, the lark springs from the soil."

"Aye, untarnished. He is"—

"Untarnished too."

"No, not untarnished. Tarnished, by no fault of his own, but still, for all that, far beneath you."

"How can one so fair be tarnished, mother?"

"I cannot tell you. It is unhappy. He is unhappy."

"If he is unhappy, I love him all the more."

"Euphrosyne, you force me to say it—he has no father."

"I have none too."

"Aye, but you had one, an honourable man."

"He is a son of the sunlight, a son of the echo. I love him."

"You shall never marry him."

"Then I will never marry at all."

"Now, Euphrosyne, do be reasonable."

"I am, mamma. It is not I who first talked or thought of marriage. You speak of it, Bianca speaks of it, Father Anselmo speaks of it. Everybody who talks to me says, 'Euphrosyne, when you are married.' The very beggar woman to whom I gave a little gift yesterday, invoked blessings on my marriage. I cannot help thinking that it is necessity since everybody speaks of it as certain. I never thought of it before. I thought I might always live here, and always have you and Bianca, and always be very happy; but since all of you have put it into my head, I have accepted the idea, and it is Charles Hauberk I love."

"Whatever for?"

"He is good, he is clever, he is sympathetical; he loves animals, he loves poetry, and he suffers. He is very, very handsome, he is a *preux chevalier*, he is a poet, and he is unhappy, and then, I love him."

"Euphrosyne, I see you are a child. I have spoken too soon. You must marry nobody yet. We will wait."

The Baroness rose, kissed her daughter, and left the room.

This is how all this had come about. The Baroness, who had really been prepossessed by Charles' appearance and manner, and was not at first indisposed to allow him to take his chance with her daughter, had been quite changed on hearing from Mr. Mangles, that indiscreet and unreflecting chatterer, all the dubious antecedents of the unhappy young man, and had been strengthened in her new opinion by hearing from de la Vigne, who, with the petty spite of weak and effeminate men, and his childish proclivity to talk, that characterises men whose brains have long lain inactive, had, fearing a dangerous rival in Charles, revealed to her the position in which he had found him in Mr. Kallandros' studio.

Now the Baroness, though a very kind woman, had innate and irradicable opinions on social matters; and it was with real pain and surprise that she had learnt how near her daughter she had allowed this young man, who was nothing better than an adventurer, to be; and she had determined to take the first opportunity to put her daughter on her guard, and was most distressed to learn how far the matter had gone. She was resolved, however, that it should go no further; and, though her heart ached for her daughter and for the young Englishman, whom she sincerely pitied, as she did it, she bade the servant give admittance to the Villa Dresda no more to Mr. Charles Hauberk.

Euphrosyne, after her mother had left the room, remained standing a little while, lost in thought; then she put her hand into her heaving bosom, and drew from the innermost folds of her dress a little bunch of withered flowers, the same that she had taken off the altar of Venus, the love-offering placed there by Charles.

These she laid on the table, and by their side, the faded letter that the dear hand of her father had written. She kissed both very tenderly, but her warm lips seemed to cling longer to the flowers. Then she said very sorrowfully—

"Poor Carlo, I love you still, whatever you be, and whatever be your faults, and I will love you always."

"The Chevalier de la Vigne," said Giovanni, throwing open the door of the room.

The Chevalier had come to have a final interview with Euphrosyne, and claim her for his bride. He had dressed himself so elegantly that he had no doubt whatever of the result. He was rather anxious, all the same, for that morning's post had brought a most pressing letter from that old *boursier*, his uncle, urging him to finish his mission and get engaged to Euphrosyne at once, adding a postscript that as the shares of the Compagnie Generale des Pots-au-feu Parisiens were so low, and that as he had almost all his fortune invested in the said Pots-au-feu, he should be unable any longer to help the young man, and that it was therefore his imperative duty to secure Euphrosyne and her *dôt* as soon as possible.

"Good morning, Euphrosyne," said the Chevalier, trying to look affectionate.

"Good morning, cousin," said Euphrosyne.

"I have come, m'demoiselle, to speak to you."

"I hope so. You would not come to be silent."

"What *esprit* you have," said the Chevalier, looking with admiration at her.

"I did not mean to show any," said Euphrosyne.

"But you did, you did, you did."

"I didn't, I didn't, I didn't."

"I love you, Euphrosyne," said the Chevalier, bringing it out at once.

Euphrosyne started; she had never taken him *au serieux*. Then she said very gravely—

"Why do you tell me this?"

That posed the Chevalier for a minute.

"Not as a compliment, I hope," continued the girl, drawing Charles' flowers to her side.

"No," said the Chevalier; "to offer you compliments would be like offering a pair of well-cut pantaloons to Dusautoy, or a bottle of jockey club to Piesse and Lubin. No; I simply mentioned the fact, to pave the way to another statement."

Euphrosyne's hand tightened over Charles' flowers. She remained silent.

"For," said the Chevalier, sitting down, after first drawing his trousers an inch above his ankles to prevent them creasing at the knees, "I have a statement to make. I have seen many things and wanted many things. I have seen rises and falls, ambition and love. I have seen a woman's downward progress from Worth's to the Boulevard des Italiens, from the Boulevard des Italiens to the Louvre, from the Louvre to the Bon Marché, from there to the Place Clichy, and so on. I have also seen men whose sole ambition in life it was to find fiacre No. 1, and drive in it. Yes, I have seen many things."

"Do you love me for that?" said Euphrosyne, smiling in spite of herself, at the absurd talk.

"I will explain," said the Chevalier. "My similes may be hard to understand. You are a woman whose progress will be upwards; you will reach Worth some day. I am a man who has higher ambitions than to ride in cab No. 1. Do you understand?"

"No more than if you spoke in Turkish," said Euphrosyne.

"I mean that we are not the ordinary people whose downward lives and foolish ambitions I have described; I mean we are suited for each other."

"What do you mean?"

"I mean that I want you to marry me. Will you?"

Euphrosyne rose, pointed to the door, and shouted rather than said—

"No."

"*Et pourquoi pas?*" said the Chevalier.

"Because no, no, no. Never."

"Are you already engaged?"

"You have no right to ask me."

"I ask it as a favour."

"Well, yes."

"To whom? Surely not to that young Englishman?"

"I do not answer more questions."

"Surely not to that young man who looks as if he *once* had credit with his tailor."

"I do not answer."

"But surely you are not serious in refusing my offer?"

"Offer? What do you offer?"

"My heart, my figure, hem—my name."

"Please, cousin, don't say anything more about it. I cannot listen to you. Please leave me."

"I will write to you from Paris."

"You will write, I hope, and I hope you will be

very happy, but don't ask me again, for I cannot, I really, really cannot."

The Chevalier bowed, left the room, and, going to the telegraph office, telegraphed to his uncle:

Pots-au feu or no Pots-au-feu, send the price of a Pullman and accessories back to Paris.

That night he received a telegram from his uncle; one single word, dating from the Bourse:

Dôt?

However he answered it, he got the money and left for Paris next day, remarking to himself as he got into the railway carriage at Naples—"Yes, I decidedly prefer Naples in *La Muette de Portici.* Dusautoy is a *blagueur* after all."

CHAPTER XV.

CAN THE LEOPARD CHANGE HIS SPOTS?

The conversation detailed in the last chapter, with Euphrosyne's subsequent interview with the Chevalier de la Vigne, took place one day after Charles's change of fortune. This young man was still in Naples, for Messrs. Turnbull & Co. would not trust him as far as £270. Bankers often will trust you for £10, but not for £100, *i.e.*, in their eyes your honesty is worth no more than £10, which reflection is not always very flattering. They had sent his cheque to their London agent, and had advanced him the sum at which they appraised his commercial value, namely, 500 francs, and with this Charles was living in splendour at his old quarters, the Hotel des Etrangers.

He did not appear at Sorrento for two weeks, and meanwhile the Baroness had received from the Baron de la Vigne, the uncle of the little Chevalier, a rather angry note:—

Paris,
Café de la Bourse.

"Dear Placide,

"Why did you not tell me before that Euphrosyne was already engaged? It would have saved me much expense and my nephew much anxiety and trouble. The poor *garçon* is very much distressed indeed, and has shaved his whiskers and has quarrelled with his tailor. Had I known that your daughter was the *fiancée* of another I would, of course, never have sent Alphonse out to Naples. I think it strange of you not to have told me.

Receive, my cousin, the expression of my very high consideration.

"Yours,
"ISIDORE.
"Baron de la Vigne,
"Ex-Courtier of the Bourse, &c., &c."

As soon as the Baroness received this note she called Euphrosyne, and showing it to her said—

"Euphrosyne, what does this mean? Did you tell your cousin that you were already engaged?"

"Yes, mamma."

"Is it true?"

"Yes."

"To whom?"

"To my father's words."

"How?"

"He bade me marry a gentleman. Alphonse was no gentleman."

"Euphrosyne?"

"No. No gentleman would have acted as he did. He owed his life to Charles Hauberk, and yet he came to you telling tales about the Englishman."

"He did quite right. He opened my eyes to the great danger of allowing this young man to be near you."

"What danger is there?"

"You know he admires you—that is the danger."

"Why?"

"Because admiration leads to love. Love often awakens responsive love. You might have learnt to love this young man, this adventurer, and then there would have been interminable annoyance to both of us."

"I tell you I do love him."

"And I tell you, Euphrosyne, you must not."

"Mother, you said I might choose as I pleased. I have chosen."

"Your father's dying words forbid you. Charles Hauberk is no gentleman."

"I cannot see why."

"Because, as I have already told you, he is of low birth."

"I am a Republican, you know, mother."

"Be it, the Republic does not excuse immorality; the Bonnet Rouge does not palliate disgrace."

"I cannot understand you when you talk of immorality and disgrace with reference to this young man."

"But they both exist."

Euphrosyne grew pale, the fire flashed from her eyes, and drawing herself up she said very slowly and very gravely—

"You are unjust."

"My daughter?"

"Yes, my mother, you are unjust. You are more, you are cruel. You are worldly. How often have you told me to hate the cold, cruel tenets of the world? How often have you professed to despise its rules? but now, where they serve you, you do not shrink from their coldness, you do not wince at their cruelty. I think I understand you. I am old enough and I have read enough to know what you mean when you speak of his disgrace, which is not his fault; of his immorality, where he is not immoral. You allow that it is not his fault, you allow that no blame is his, and yet you join with the world in condemning, contemning, and rejecting him. In what are you better than the world?"

The Baroness listened quietly, casting glances of love and admiration at her beautiful daughter, while she spoke so bravely. Then she rose and kissed her, saying—

"No better than the world, my child, no better; but brought up to certain principles we cannot reject them. They form part of us, and we can no more unlearn them than we can unlearn the rules of social etiquette."

"But you see their injustice?"

"Yes, as clearly as I see the absurdity of several social rules. Still I cannot practise according to my perception in either case."

"Why not?"

"Because, first, I am Placide, daughter of General the Baron de Granmont; secondly, widow of the Baron de Bienamée; thirdly, because I am known in society; finally, because I am your mother."

"Because you are my mother you should let me be happy; because you are known in society you should show society that it is wrong; because you are the Baroness de Bienaimée, *née* de Granmont, you should have ideas above those of the people."

"By reason of my position I can not see you united to a man beneath you in caste, utterly removed from your class."

"But he may rise above it."

"He cannot. A negro can never become white."

"But a pariah may cleanse himself."

"A pariah of society, never."

"Why?"

"I don't know, it has always been so."

"It has always been so. That is what the nobles answered to the complaining peasants before '91. They rose, and cast off the shackling 'Whatever is, is right.'"

The Baroness did not feel herself able to continue the argument. She knew that she could never be brought to see the matter in this light, she knew that she could never allow her daughter to marry an illegitimate child, and she saw also how liberally-minded Euphrosyne had grown, so she rose, saying—

"I cannot argue with you, Euphrosyne. Remember that I am your mother."

With that she withdrew.

"I do, I do," said Euphrosyne, sinking into a chair. "But I love him, I love him, I love him."

"Euphrosyne?"

Bianca had entered and stood in the doorway.

"Yes, Bianca," said Euphrosyne, rising.

"What troubles you?"

"Nothing."

"But, little sister," said Bianca, coming forward and throwing her arm round the girl's neck, "you are sorry. I see tears in your eyes. What grieves you?"

"That the pariah may never cleanse himself."

"What pariah?"

"The pariah of society. Mother told me so."

"I met the Baroness just now. She seemed *froissée*. Do you know what I heard her tell Giovanni."

"What?"

"She said, 'Remember, Giovanni, that Mr. Hauberk is never to come here again.'"

"Bianca?"

"Yes, Euphrosyne; I was so surprised, and so sorry. I thought the Baroness liked Charles very much."

Bianca looked perplexed. She was not quite so wise as her friend, and, to tell the truth, did not quite know what a pariah was. The word was connected vaguely in her mind with white oxen and jungles.

"Listen to me, Bianca," continued Euphrosyne, drawing her friend down to her side on the sofa. "I want to talk to you. Suppose your mother was alive, and suppose you loved her very much, and suppose you also loved a man very much, and that your mother did not like this man because of his social position, and refused to let you love him; but that you did love him very much"—

"I should love him all the more," said a voice at the open window.

The girls started and turned. It was Charles Hauberk.

The young man had just returned from Naples. He had got his money, and was quite happy again. He had come straight to the Villa Dresda; and hearing voices in the drawing-room had come up to the open window.

"I beg your pardon, ladies," he continued, bowing, "I have only come back from Naples to-day, and I came straight here to pay you my respects. I saw the drawing-room window open, so I came up to it," then, seeing the deep blush on Euphrosyne's cheeks, he added hastily, "I have heard but little of what you said. I hope my joke does not hurt you."

Euphrosyne was about to reply, when Giovanni entered with a letter. He saw Charles before he retired.

Bianca looked at Euphrosyne, and said in a low voice—

"What will the Baroness say?"

Charles was continuing his apologies for his ill-timed appearance, when Giovanni, coming round to where he stood, told him that the Baroness desired to speak to him at once.

"Certainly," said Charles, "with pleasure."

Giovanni showed him into the Baroness's private sitting-room, and asked him to sit down.

Presently Madame de Bienaimée came into the room. Charles bowed to her; she motioned him to sit down again.

She seated herself, and taking up some embroidery began to work, as if perplexed how to begin.

Charles said, "Giovanni told me you wanted to speak to me."

"Yes," answered the Baroness.

Then, after a pause, she handed the piece of embroidery that she had been working at to Charles. It was a design of the Bienaimée arms, worked on canvas, for a cushion.

She said, "Can you read that motto?"

"Yes," said Charles. "*Notre honneur avant notre vie.* A beautiful motto."

"It is a beautiful motto," said the Baroness. "Do you believe that in some families the motto of their coat of arms is the principle of their lives?"

"Certainly," said Charles, "though in my case I am afraid I do not follow our motto. 'For King and State' is the Hauberk motto, and I am rather Republican."

These words of Charles' rather helped the lady out of her difficulty, for she felt rather angry at his apparent duplicity in styling himself a Hauberk, when she knew his name to be Benson, and thinking more of him as an impudent impostor, she felt that she need not use so much delicacy towards him in saying what she had to say.

"In *our* family," she answered, "in the

Bienaimée family, honour has always been held before life. My husband died to defend his honour."

Charles bowed.

"He was the last Bienaimée," continued the Baroness, "and his daughter is the only remaining representative of our family. She is still very young, and perhaps not circumspect. I have therefore to watch over her."

Charles' heart beat high. He waited for the Baroness to continue.

"I have to see, also, that those principles which have been part and parcel of the family ever since Charles VIII. allowed them to engrave them in the form of a motto on their coat-of-arms, are duly respected by my child."

"What can be coming?" thought Charles, as he bowed once more in acquiescence.

"Now honour proceeds from within, and comes from without. The honour of a family while resting on its deeds, will not be complete unless that family is respected. Respect from the world is also the honour of a family. Do you understand my meaning?"

"Perfectly," answered Charles.

"I have therefore to see that the respect in which the Bienaimée family has for so many centuries been held by the world is not weakened or destroyed, and that this is not brought about by the unconsidered action of a thoughtless child."

"I do not think such a thing possible," said Charles.

"But it is possible, it is probable, it is imminent," said the Baroness, nerving herself.

"Am I an accomplice in bringing about so great a disaster?" said Charles, who at last began to have a dim perception of the drift of her words.

"Not directly," said Madame de Bienaimée, wishing to spare him, "but it is with reference to this matter that I wish to speak to you. I have to forbid you the house."

"Madame?"

"I believe you admire my daughter; I know that she is not indifferent to you. I also know"—

"Stay, madame," said Charles, rising to his feet, his cheeks glowing, and with flashing eyes, "I will finish it all for you. You are quite right. Your daughter is a Bienaimée, and I am a bastard. I am worse than that, I am a bastard without decency. I proclaim my shame from the housetops. Discontented with hiding beneath the *bourgeois* name of Benson, so kindly provided for me by those who had to discard me, I take the name of Hauberk, to which I have no right. You are perfectly right. Then, I am an adventurer. I made debts and ran away from Oxford. I live by my wits, now as a ferryman, now as an artist's model. That is what you wanted to say to me. I have spared you the trouble."

"You put your unhappy case in a very much worse light than the one I look at it in, my poor boy," said the Baroness, tenderly. "I am very, very sorry for your misfortune, I regret that you should have been led to commit actions unworthy of a man, but you must allow that, as all this is so, I am not justified in allowing you to visit my daughter."

Charles stood still, quite silent, but suffocating with suppressed emotion.

"You see," continued the Baroness, in a most kind tone of voice, "that my daughter is the representative of one of our greatest French families, and as such must not marry anyone whose own birth will not bear the strongest investigation. I have to see to that. The honour of our family requires it. In time I could overlook the childish extravagances and errors which have led to a life of penury, and to work which, though not disreputable, is not the occupation of a gentleman. But, as the mother of Euphrosyne, daughter of Gilleroy de Bienaimée, I cannot overlook"—

"The bar sinister," said Charles.

"Yes."

"You are quite right, madam," said Charles, bowing. "It is true I love your daughter. This is an impertinence on my part. Still, I have read of a leper who loved, and, they say, he loved well and truly, and that his love was so beautiful and pure that the lady forgot his uncleanliness, and took his hand, and, braving the world, went forth with him happy in his love. They even say that the garb of leprosy hid in him an angel from heaven. That of course is only a story. I will go away from here. I will never cross your path again; but the leper will love the lady still."

"I thought it best to separate you before it grew too late," said the Baroness. "I am pained and distressed more than I can say, to see the pain you suffer. I earnestly pray and hope you will have a happy life, and become a good, brave man; but you must learn to forget my daughter."

"I will leave Sorrento to-day," said Charles.

"Not on my account," said the Baroness, "there is no need for that. We are going to Florence for a season, and when we come back, if you will promise to be discreet in your behaviour to Euphrosyne, you will always be welcome to me. For," said she, going up to him and laying her hand tenderly on his shoulder, "you are a gentleman in spite of all, and a very high-principled one. I wish things were not so cruel."

Charles took her hand and kissed it. Then he bowed and went away, well-nigh heart-broken.

Thus ended the interview.

CHAPTER XVI.

A NEWSPAPER PARAGRAPH.

Anyone reading the London newspapers about this time, must have remarked, in the police news columns, the following paragraph :—

"A Singular Case.—At the Mansion House, yesterday, a woman, giving the name of Esther only, and refusing to state her age or address, respectably dressed, was charged before Alderman Sir Thomas Whatnot, with being a lunatic at large. On Tuesday morning the defendant stopped a policeman in Fleet Street, and complained to him that her husband had stolen her peace of mind. The officer saw her again later on in the Temple, and from her demeanour and conversation was induced to take her in custody for protection's sake. Evidence was given by Drs. William Guller and Joseph Venibles, of her insanity. Mr. Snorker, corndealer, said he had known defendant at Exeter by the name of Jane Smith. She had been always excitable and eccentric. In answer to the inquiries of his worship, witness replied that he had known her in the capacity of laundress. He had met her in London, and she had told him she was married, but that her gold locket had gone and she could not find it. He had taken her to Drs. Guller and Venibles, who had both certified her to be of unsound mind. He did this purely out of charity.

Did not know defendant's address at Exeter, or if she had any friends there. Defendant would not answer any questions, and Sir Thomas Whatnot accordingly ordered her to be sent to Peckham Lodge Lunatic Asylum, where she would be well and kindly treated."

CHAPTER XVII.

"HARLOT MOTHER! I CURSE YOU."

BEATEN down in heart and spirit, wounded in the most sensitive part of his sensitive nature, and doubly wounded by the kind way in which the truth, which he recognized only too well, had been put to him, deprived suddenly of all hope, at the very moment when hope seemed to be the least misplaced, stung to the quick by a feeling of bitter shame, Charles slunk rather than walked as he made his way out of the grounds of the Villa Dresda.

Never to see Euphrosyne again, never to watch her pretty child-like face turned on him with admiration, never again to have her restless eyes, which he alone could enchain, fixed with the faint beginnings of an absorbing love on him, never to see her smile, never any more to hear her laugh, never to feel any more that he of all men had the power to amuse, to interest, to cheer, to charm the radiant girl that he loved so well, never, never any more. No hope, no shadow of a hope.

The black raven, the *sinistra cornix*, the blighting shadow of whose sombre wings had thrown a perpetual gloom over his life, had croaked forth to him in tones which there was no mistaking. "Never more, never more."

"Were it not for the bar sinister that defaces

your coat-of-arms you would not be unwelcome to me." This was the gist of the lady's words.

Were it not. Were it not. But it is.

Nothing could undo that, no Papal bull even, no sign manual of the vicar of Christ could rescind the excommunication spoken by the world out against the children of a natural birth.

He could not alter it, nothing could alter it. Nothing could disprove it.

His father was dead, buried beneath a weight of marble slabs, whereon, in gilded letters and sonorous prose, his many virtues, his many worldly honours were engraven; whence he could never rise to claim his son, and say to the poor boy—

"This is my well-beloved son, begotten of me, and no son of the people, no *filius nullius.*"

And his mother, she was lost, or if, indeed, she was living, to find her would be to bring more disgrace on to himself. Some boorish peasant wench, may be, or worse, some cheap actress flaunting on the dirty boards of the stage of some London gaff; still boasting to her envious companions of the old days of her old triumphs, of the noble my lord she had once enthralled, perhaps now the mistress of some low vagabond, some infamous *souteneur*, on whom she would play off the old wiles, on whom she would lavish the same smiles, the same caresses, which had brought the house of Hauberk so very, very low.

At this thought Charles balled his fist, and cried in a voice hoarse with passion—

"*Harlot mother! I curse you.*"

Towards his father, of course, as is the way of the world, he had no evil thoughts; he reverenced his name, the splendour of his ultra-Conquest ancestry, his well-known character of an old sporting Tory, of a good landlord, of a brave gentleman. Lord Hauberk had in his day been the most popular of all English noblemen, and his Melton prowess and Paris gallantry had been the theme of admiring conversation all over the kingdom. Patron of the ring, breeder of three Derby winners, and the best race of fox terriers that existed, he represented the personified attainment of the height of worldly ambition, and his death, leaving no direct heir, had caused much regret in fashionable circles, who were loth to see the splendid manor of Appledean pass into the hands of a distant cousin, whose claim the lawyers had had to trace back to the time of King Charles II., an old philosopher, who hated fox-hunting, and allowed his keepers to shoot down *sitting* pheasants when he wanted game for his table. His want of issue too was a source of fashionable regret, for the haute aristocracy contemplated with melancholy the total extinction of the grand old family name. The Earldom of Brookshire was no more, and now shortly the Barony of Hauberk was to be erased from the roll of English titles. Nor was this regret an idle one, for with what disgust do the members of our aristocracy see the numbers of their peers daily increased by the shoddiest of men, and see coronets which were formerly only distributed for great loyalty or brave deeds, flung in handfuls amongst the mushroom men of yesterday.

With fretful thoughts like these did Charles occupy his teeming mind as he walked away from the Villa Dresda, through Sorrento and along the Massa road. He loved this road, not so much for its rare beauty but for the fact that here he had first been in Euphrosyne's company alone. How long ago that seemed, when he thought of all the phases of emotion through which he had passed, and how short, as a span of happiness. How changed too was his position. Then he was in a desperate state of poverty, and now he had a fair competence once more, but how willingly would he have changed his position for the old adventurous, needy, one, and be once more allowed to hope, as he had hoped then, that some day he might find happiness where his happiness alone lay.

"Ah," cried he, for the thought came to him that perhaps Euphrosyne too had turned away from him, and that she too was one of the prejudiced ones.

"Yet, oh yet, thyself deceive not,
Love may sink by slow decay,
But by sudden wrench, believe not
Hearts can thus be torn away.

"Still thine own its life retaineth,
Still must mine, tho' bleeding, beat,
And the undying thought which paineth
Is—that we no more may meet."

And at these words, tears that blotted too the paper on which the trembling hand first wrote them, came to his eyes, and in an agony of grief he threw himself on the bank, and buried his face in his hands.

Now it so happened that Euphrosyne had chosen this road for her walk, and presently she came by, and when she saw Charles lying there she fancied he was asleep, for he made no movement and still lay there, his face buried in his hands.

She had a habit of talking aloud what thoughts occupied her mind, and, as she stood looking at the form of him she loved, she spake and said; half to herself, and half addressing him—

"It was here we met, and it is here we have to part. It was here my heart first burst into life, and it is here my heart must break. How cruel to love, and never to know my love has been returned, and not to be allowed to know, to be taken away from him, before I have ever heard the real echoes of his heart, before I have ever felt his kiss, the kiss I yearn for; and yet this is to be, for to-morrow we leave, and I do not know when we return. Poor boy, I wonder whether he sleeps. Yes, he is asleep, and there, as I gently remove his hands from his face I see the marks of tears, and those dear lips which I so long to kiss are drawn as if in pain. He has suffered, I know, and at my mother's hands, at the hands of her I have always loved, but cannot love so well as I love him. Oh, if I might lie down by his side, and take him in my arms, and kiss him, and lie there with him always on that bed of flowers, with the silvery olive-leaves overhead for our canopy, and all the beauty of the world around us, and that he might never wake, but in his dreams whisper my name linked with some word of love, that I might know the depth of his heart. Oh, Carlo, Carlo, I love you."

And taking from her dress a flower, it was a rose, she bent tenderly over him and placed it in his bosom.

"A lady did that once," she whispered, "for a poet whom she knew not, and I do it for one I know and one whom I love. And it will be my happiness if he thinks of my token, as did the blind singer of England."

Then, looking at him a space, with eyes full of love, and as if hesitating whether to kiss his upturned face right gently, and then to steal quietly away.

But hush! he was speaking, speaking in his sleep—

"I love you, I love you. Do you know what that means? And the undying thought that paineth is that we no more may meet. Say, Euphrosyne, the outcast can love, the pariah has a heart. You do not believe it. You are but of the world, but for all that I love—you." Then he was silent, and Euphrosyne stood with her hand pressed against her heart.

Suddenly he woke, and after looking vaguely at the blushing form before him, recognized the girl.

He rose, and bowed very distantly, then he said—

"Signorita, leave the leper to himself, I carry infection with me."

"You are no leper to me," said Euphrosyne.

"But to your mother I am," answered Charles, and then, starting forward as driven by an irresistible impulse, "but I will tell you, lady, I love you."

Euphrosyne looked straight into his eyes, and putting out her hand, said very lovingly—

"Yes, Carlo, you told me so before. Just now, you were asleep, you know, you spoke of me. I could not help listening, could I? I was happy, very happy, and I am happy now, for I love you too, very dearly."

Charles looked round, and, seeing that nobody was in sight, sprang forward, and taking the blushing girl in his arms, pressed her passionately to his heart and covered her face, hands, and neck with kisses.

"My angel, my angel," he cried. "I love you, and have ever since I first saw you standing in radiant beauty that moonlit night. I have no thoughts which do not turn to thee. Thou hast made me happy, suffer, go mad, enter the highest feelings of pleasure, in turn. And now you tell me that you love me, and the words which but yesterday would have made me the happiest and gladdest of men, seem but a cruel irony to-day. I may never meet you on the old terms again. To-day, your mother bade me cease my visits to you, and said that she was going to take you away to Florence, and I shall never see you again, and, if I suffered before, what must I suffer now that I know that you love me. Oh! it is cruel to lose you now, Euphrosyne."

"You do not lose me," said Euphrosyne, timidly putting her arms round his neck, and laying her head on his bosom. "You shall never lose me, I will love you always."

"If you love me," said Charles bitterly, "tell me not of it. Tell me you hate me, and I will then find life offers me a task to do. But loving me, as things stand now, is like pointing out a promised land to a sightless man."

"How cruel you are," said Euphrosyne, reproachfully. "I cannot help my mother's actions, I cannot get her to see things with my eyes; all I can do is to love you, and I do, my darling, very, very much."

Charles bent down to her lips, and pressed his to them, for a long while, then he said—

"Time is a kindly god, and cures most things. I will be content for a little while to lose you. The possession afterwards will be all the more precious. But you must remember to love me very much always, as much as I shall love you, and you will write to me, and I will write to you, and we will try and content ourselves with this, till a day comes, as it will come, my Euphrosyne, when I may claim you in the face of the world as my wife."

"I am all yours, and I will do whatever you wish," said Euphrosyne; then, after a pause, she added, "Will you stay here, Carlo?"

"No, Euphrosyne, I love Sorrento, and could well pass away years of my life here, but that is because you were here. I could not stay here now, to wander forlornly about, and call you by name, and pause, and wait for an answer, and yet know that the answer would never, never come. Each spot here is hallowed in my mind by some recollection of you, and by that recollection only, and to stay here after you have gone, would be like one gazing on the empty frame, whence some ruthless hand has stolen the portrait of his dear lady. No. I have idled too long, and now 'tis the season of work, and my happiness will be to know that now I am really working for you. Oh, Euphrosyne, we shall be happy together."

"I am never happy but when I am near you," said Euphrosyne.

Then they fell to talking as lovers always do, talking and giving caresses, uttering and responding words of endearment, and time went lightly by. It was not till evening that they parted, and they had promised to write, and to be faithful to each other, and to feed the flame of their love with the kindling hope to be together for ever some day. And the sun went down in glory behind the purple isles, and the sky and sea were all aflame with brilliant light, and the white olive trees threw a dark shade, as their lips met for the last time.

CHAPTER XVIII.

TRUE HEARTS ARE MORE THAN CORONETS.

In a few days the pleasant little society that had grouped round the hospitable house of the Baroness de Bienaimée was broken up and scattered in different directions.

The Baroness, accompanied by Euphrosyne and Bianca, departed for Florence, and after their departure Charles could no longer stay at Sorrento. Mangles had gone back to England, after having done Charles as much mischief as he well could. Charles had had an interview with him at the Tramontano, the same evening that he had bade Euphrosyne a last good-night. Mangles professed himself glad to see him, but Charles cut him short by flinging down a cheque for £150, and bidding him give him a receipt and hold his peace.

"I am in no humour," he had said, "to put up with your vulgarity, and I wish to say that I hope that now all intercourse between us will stop. You have been a stumbling-block to me many times, and now that you have no claims on me—you will observe I have calculated the interest due on your loan—I must request you to forget that we were ever acquainted."

Mangles had answered by crushing the cheque up in his hand and throwing it into the corner, and then signed the receipt. (A rather crumpled cheque for £150, payable by the Penrith Bank to Mr. Mangles was, let it be added, shortly afterwards passed through the London clearing-house.)

Charles then went home to his lodgings, and drew up and sent to the *Oxford Guardian* and *Oxford Chronicle* the following advertisement :—

NOTICE.—All Tradesmen having claims upon Mr. Charles Hauberk (Benson), late of St. Mary's College, are requested to send in a statement of such claims on or before Wednesday, the 14th inst., for payment. No letters from solicitors can be entertained, and, if sent in, will not be answered. — Address, CHARLES HAUBERK, The Grande Sentinelle Hotel, Sorrento, Golfo di Napoli.

In about eight days Charles was favoured with a shower of bills, the first to come in being that of The Spider, who had written across the back—"Mr. Harrison begs to call the special attention of Mr. Hauberk to the sweet things in summer trowserings which he has in stock; also to a few cases of Havanna cigars, at £5 the box.—P.S. Twelve months' credit, or ten per cent. discount for cash within three months."

Charles paid all his bills, and felt greatly relieved at being no longer under any obligation to men of the Harrison type, so rightly nicknamed after the insect that never looses its prey till its victim's last drop of blood has been sucked out. When these matters were at last settled he began to think what he should do, and how to best employ his talents and his £2,000. He had, it is true, first had the idea of following Euphrosyne to

Florence, but his sense of honour and of the consideration due to the Baroness, prevented him; and yet he felt very miserable wandering about alone, for having declined the friendship and society of the Mertons, and by having, in doing so, practically renounced the society of Herbert Lovell, when he did not need it, he felt too proud to seek it now. Often the poor boy would wander up to the Villa Dresda gate, and press his face against the cold iron bars, and strain his eyes gazing on the ground where he had first spoken to the dear girl he so fondly loved; and often, too, he would call "Euphrosyne, Euphrosyne!" What times the hum of the buzzing gadfly, or, at eventide, the wanton chirping of the cicada, would alone respond!

At last he could stand it no longer, and determined to go back to England, and after a little reflection decided on doing so. He went, therefore, to tell Herbert and bid him good-bye. Herbert was as usual with the Mertons, and when Charles entered he found his friend in a very affectionate pose with Mildred, while Brother John looked on, beaming with happy smiles.

Charles bowed to the Mertons, and addressing Herbert, said—"I've come to say good-bye, Herbert."

"Good-bye, Charles?"

"Yes; I am leaving in a day or two for England."

"Oh, Charles," said Herbert, "why did you not tell me so before?'

"I have only just decided on doing so. Plans are quickly formed with me."

"Then you are really decided," said Herbert.

"Yes."

"Well, let me help you with your things—to pack, and so on."

Charles readily availed himself of his friend's offer, and while they were so engaged Herbert said—

"Charles, do you look on me as a friend?"

Charles disliked exhibitions of sentiment and sentimental phrases, so he answered rather abruptly, and consequently without much grace—

"Yes, yes, of course; why do you ask?"

"Because," said Herbert gravely, "I want to tell you something which will interest you, and yet I fear to pain you."

"What is it," said Charles, sitting down on his portmanteau with an air of resignation.

Herbert put a letter into his hands and said—

"I have loved you, Charles, very much, and now I am forbidden, by the only person whose authority I acknowledge, to have any intercourse with you."

"Indeed?"

"Yes, Charles, that letter is from my mother; I wish you to read it, and, if you can, to give me an explanation of its contents. I cannot obey it, for I love you, my friend, and yet I want an explanation. There is some mistake, I am certain."

"Perhaps this letter will not be a very pleasant one for me to read, and as I dislike sentimentalities of any sort, I must ask you to excuse me from reading this letter."

"No, no," said Herbert, anxiously. "I want you to read it. It alters nothing. There is a mistake."

"As you wish it," said Charles, "I will do it."

Charles then unfolded the letter. It dated from Havre, and announced the arrival of Mrs. Dixon, Herbert's mother, at that port. After sundry observations on financial matters, and on her passage from New York, the writer paragraphed off as follows:—

"You tell me now for the first time that you have a friend named Charles Hauberk, and that he is staying with you at Sorrento, and that you will be very glad to introduce him to me. This is what I say. Loathe the man who bears that name as you loathe an unclean thing, as you loathe folly, treachery, vice, deceit and liars. If you love your mother, sunder at once all connection with him and shun him as you would a leper. I cannot come to Sorrento while he is there. I could not come within a hundred miles of him. Therefore choose; either abandon your friend or be content never to see me again. Unless I hear that you have done as I wish, I shall take the next mail back to America. Either get rid of your friend, and come and meet me at Paris, or renounce all hope of ever seeing me again."

"What can it mean?" said Herbert, pained to see how deeply his friend was wounded.

"Mean? ah—mean? And you say that this interesting, lady-like epistle was written by"—

"Dora Dixon, my mother," said Herbert.

"Dora Dixon, indeed, widow of the late"—

"John Dixon, brewer of Surat beer, at New York," said Herbert, rather piqued by his friend's manner.

"Oh, a brewer. Well, well, perhaps that explains it," said Charles, with the greatest insolence, and hardly knowing what he was saying.

"Yes, never mind that, but tell me, Charles, what do you think it means?" said Herbert affectionately, and making every allowance for his friend's feelings.

"Mean? How can I know. The lady apparently dislikes the aristocracy of England, and therefore includes the bearer of one of its names. I cannot offer to explain the line of reasoning she pursued in penning these lines, I have not the lady's acquaintance, and do not desire it. All I can say is, that I can, of course, not be the reason that so polite a lady and so loving a son should be separated, and all I can do is to wish you a very good day."

Now there are limits to all human tempers, and Charles's tone was even more insolent than his expressions. Herbert, who had been quite startled, and, in no ordinary measure, pained on reading the letter which he had only that very morning received, had made the amplest allowance, for Charles's *amour-propre*, and the pride which he knew was his besetting sin; but hearing his mother insulted, and not seeing in his natural anger that the effect of the letter had quite bereft Charles of any discernment or consideration, he could contain himself no longer, and said in some anger—

"You shall not insult my mother. I will not allow it."

"I had no intention of insulting Mrs. Do-ra Di-xon, as I believe she is called. The insult seems to be on her side."

"I tell you I will not allow it."

"You will not allow what?"

"I will not allow you to insult my mother. I gave you the letter to read, telling you there was a mistake. You make no allowances."

"I can make no allowances for such a letter. The letter is the worst specimen of"—

"I tell you to be quiet."

"Indeed, *you* tell *me* to be quiet. Mr. Lovell, you are as unreasonable as—"

"Have you no feeling?" cried Herbert. "Have you no gentlemanly honour?"

"I answer no questions," said Charles, starting to his feet, and pointing to the door.

Herbert looked at him, his blood was up. And yet he loved his friend well, and was sick at heart at this unseemly quarrel.

Charles was utterly disgusted with himself at what he had been saying, but perverseness had got hold of him, and spoke from his lips, while his whole body winced at the cruel words he himself uttered.

Perhaps Herbert noticed this, for he grew calm and said—

"I can understand your anger. It is not unnatural. It is not illegitimate as you are"—

"You are a mean, damned scoundrel," said Charles, starting forward in a burst of rage, "You are the lowest of blackguards. Take that," and he struck him with all his force on the mouth.

Charles had not marked his friend's altered tone, but had only heard the words—"It is not illegitimate as you are"—and did not wait, but, driven by perverseness, and probably knowing all the while in his heart of hearts that Herbert had never meant his words as a reproach, but was only beginning a sentence, had sprung forward and done his cruel deed.

He raised his arm to strike again, but Herbert caught his arm, and said—

"Are you mad, Charles? What have you done?"

"What I will repeat," said Charles; "what I will do to chastise everyone who insults me."

"Do you know whom you have struck?"

"Aye, well enough, Herbert Lovell."

"You have struck"—began Herbert; then he paused and looking sorrowfully at Charles, put his handkerchief to his bleeding mouth, and walked slowly to the door. There he paused and said—"You will be very sorry some day, Charles. I wish you a true good-bye."

"Get away," said Charles, through his teeth.

The door opened, and Herbert went out. The

next minute Charles threw himself on his bed and gave way to a passion of grief and a flood of burning tears.

In a few moments he jumped up, and struck himself with his balled fist in the face, and again, and again, and then he ran to the door and cried—

"Herbert, Herbert, come back!"

But Herbert was out of hearing, and they met no more.

That evening Charles left the Grande Sentinelle, and took the Florio-Rubattino steamer to Genoa, which he reached the following morning. He was driven to an hotel, and the first thing he did was to write the two following letters:—

To Mr. Herbert Lovell, Sorrento.

"My Dear Herbert,

"Forgive me. I cannot excuse my behaviour. I must have been mad. I misunderstood what you said. I was very sorry immediately afterwards.

"Your very affectionate,

"C. Hauberk."

To Mademoiselle Euphrosyne de Bienaimée, Lungarno, Firenze.

"My own Darling Little Euphrosyne,

"You see I have left Sorrento. I could not bear it after you had left, and so I went too. I wanted very much to come to Florence after you, but thought it might vex the Baroness, as indeed it would have done. Is Mademoiselle Bianca with you? Do you know, I met her the morning you left, and she looked very strangely at me, and all she said was, 'Hope,' and, indeed, Hope is all I live on—hope some day to have you for ever. My pretty little darling, I cannot tell you how much I am looking forward to your first letter. Be sure to write it in English.

"Oh, I forgot; I have such a droll thing to tell. I bought the Paris *Figaro* to-day, and saw a paragraph called *La Marée et Le Mari* in the gossip column, under the heading, *Carnet d'un Mondain*, which seems to refer to the Chevalier de la Vigne; and as I believe he was my rival, I send you the cutting, to show you to what heroic deeds the love of you can drive men.

[The cutting, freely translated, is as follows:—A few months ago, the fraternity of *boulevardiers* lost one of their members, a man who was the most regular at the *heure d' absinthe*, and the *heure du vermouth*, and who was always to be seen between three and five o'clock driving in the Bois with the *fameuse equestrienne* of the Hippodrome, Mme. C. There was much grief among this *côterie*, and nobody knew what had become of him. He has suddenly reappeared, and is mute to all questions as to where he has been. I am, however, informed that this gentleman has been on a pilgrimage to Cythera, the object of his passion being a young lady, daughter of a very old and aristocratic Bourbon family, who resides with her mother in a coquet villa not far from N—, in Italy. I am also informed that the lady's *dôt* is very considerable, and would by no means have been unwelcome to the young man, who, as it may be remembered, lost rather heavily over *Café au lait* at the Auteuil races last spring. He was, however, unsuccessful in his wooing, and planned a terrible revenge, nothing less than to prove his love and wound his cruel love's heart by a melodramatic suicide. Imitating the hero of Victor Hugo's romance, *Les Travailleurs de la Mer,* he chose a rock in full view of the Villa Dresda, and sat there waiting for the cruel sea to engulf him and his miseries. But the *sacré* Mediterranean was not *en accord*, and refused the shelter of her bosom to the luckless, lovelorn young man. After waiting five hours for the tide to rise, he abandoned his seat, and his project, in disgust, and thus a valuable life has been spared, and the *restaurateurs* of the Boulevards have once more among their *clientèle un fameux consommateur*.]

"Fancy the poor little Chevalier waiting for the tide of the tideless sea—is it not droll?

"I shall be here some time, and then go on to Venice. Write soon, and believe me, with a thousand kisses, ever your devoted lover,

"CHARLES HAUBERK."

CHAPTER XIX.

LOST.

Correspondence between Charles Hauberk and Euphrosyne de Bienaimée, and others:—

"My Dearest Charles,

"If I could write to you every day I would, for nothing gives me more pleasure than to commune with you even through the silent medium of a letter; but I am obliged to be very careful, for I know that mamma would be displeased if she knew that I was writing to you. Therefore also, I ask you, though my heart aches to do so, not to write every day as you have done all this month. Mamma sees all the letters that come into the house, and as it is not very usual for me to receive so many letters, she will become suspicious, and perhaps forbid me to write to you or receive your letters.

"I am not very happy, and but for your dear letters and the love that speaks forth from every line, I should be very miserable. I feel certain that mamma knows that I still love you, and is so opposed to it that she is doing her best to marry me to the Duke, Arnolfo, you know, the brother of dear Bianca, whom, as a child, and before I met you, I fancied I could love. He is here constantly, and I believe he wishes to court me. I do not like him the least bit now, for my eyes have been opened, and I cannot love such a man.

"Bianca is very kind to me, and it is to her I confide my secrets, and it is to her every night in my chamber that I talk of you; she speaks so well of you, and I am sure will use all her influence with her brother to prevent him from troubling me.

"I will write to you again as soon as I hear that you have reached Venice, and now, with all my heart, I wish you a happy good-night; oh, if I might be near you now!—A loving kiss.

"Tua Sposa,

"EUPHROSYNE."

"Venice.

"MY OWN DARLING EUPHROSYNE,

"Your letter, which reached me on the eve of my departure, gave me pain. I cannot tell you how anxious I feel when I hear from you that you are forced to be with the Duca di Caserta, while I am far away from you. Surely your mother will never force you to marry a man whom you cannot love. I can say nothing against the Duke. I liked what I saw of him very much. He is brave and handsome, and has the worldly recommendation of possessing a princely fortune, and an unstained name. But he is not the man to pick my little flower and hold it in his hot grasp. Did I ever read you my lines—

The lily quivers in the peasant's grasp,
  The aspen shivers in the cold north wind,
The gilded moth within the eager clasp
  Leaves of its beauty not a trace behind.

You are a tender lily, and not made to bloom in the hot breath of the world. Oh, Euphrosyne, when I think of the happiness that would be mine, to live in the same secluded spot of beauty with you, and to be with you always where never harm or hurt might befall you, and where we should live in and for ourselves alone. When will that day come? When, when?

"I cannot obey your injunction about writing, but if you wish I will not post my letters each day, but write every day and send them off together in one envelope at the end of the week. They will be very similar. I can tell you nothing but that I love you, and love you, and love you.

"I shall not be at Venice very long. I want to go back to England. I want to clear up this mystery about my birth. I want to be certain one way or other if I am a pariah, or, after all, a respectable citizen. If I find, as I know I shall, that I am what the world holds me to be, I shall come to you at once and take your decision. In the other case I shall be an ordinary mortal, and must take my chance with your mother. I will write again before I leave.

"With undying love I remain, my own sweet girl,

"Your loving and devoted

"CHARLES HAUBERK."

Letter from Herbert Lovell, Sorrento (Forwarded from Genoa):—

"MY DEAREST CHARLES,

"I received your note from Genoa, and would have answered it at once, but when I am in anger with a person, I like to test my own feelings before writing on impulse. There was, however, little need for me to follow my rule in this case, for I have never borne you the least ill-will. I was very sorry at what had happened, and very glad that I controlled my feelings. Your blow was decidedly hard, I should not have thought you could have hit so well. It is a great gift is hard hitting in these days, where everybody, thinking themselves protected by the law, are as insolent as they can be. Well, let us say nothing more about it.

"My mother is now staying at Sorrento. She has been here three weeks, and is charmed with the place. She bears you as much ill-will as ever, and will not hear your name mentioned. She has forbidden me ever to speak about you, and when I asked her why, she got very angry and spoke quite harshly to me. It is a sad mystery. I so much wanted you to know her. She is so kind and gentle as a rule, and would, I know, have grown very fond of you, and replaced, perhaps, the mother you have lost.

"And now, dear Charles, let me preach. You said once something which pained me very much. Do you remember? It was just after I heard the news of my stepfather's death. I asked you if you loved your mother dearly, and you said—'But for the fact that I am alive, I have no proof

I ever had a mother. No, I have no reason to cherish her memory. Her legacy was to me one of grief, of tears, of reproach. I never knew her —my happiness lies there.' I felt very sorry when I heard you speak thus, for whatever her fault or whatever her life, she was and is still your mother. Just think of the word, mother, what a holy sound it has. How true were the words of my poor countryman—

Because I feel that in the heavens above,
The angels whispering to one another,
Can find among their burning words of love
None so devotional as that of ' mother.'

"From all you have said about yourself, I cannot help knowing what it is that grieves you every day, but why turn your resentment on your mother ; the woman is always the less culpable in those matters, and bears all the shame, and all the suffering. And you should not, even in your thoughts, be one of those who condemn her. Be certain she loved you, oh, she loved you, and no doubt her last thoughts, when hunted from the world, broken-hearted with shame and suffering, she laid herself down for the last time, were of her dear boy, and those lips so soon to become cold in death, kissed you, and kissed you, and whispered with her last breath a prayer for you.

"I think my inferences have been correct and may tell you I have often thought of your position with great pain in *one* direction and hope and consolation in another. In the presence of a great grief, my lips have sometimes remained silent.

'The heart knoweth its own bitterness, and a stranger intermeddleth not with its joy,' says Solomon. I feel, in wishing to console you, how very possible it is to be *cruel* in the attempt to administer *comfort.* But there are some people in the world who are only legitimate in point of birth and illegitimate in every other thing almost, and fully alive to the disadvantages and the pain of your position, all the greater and the more intense by reason of your education and social position, I say this, and I mean what I say, that your heart being turned to good, I would rather, by one hundred times, be *you*, than plenty of legitimate gentlemen, and those even far from being what the world would stigmatise as scoundrels. Nothing really disgraces a man but bad conduct, and the very fact that your position is a painful one in a certain sense, would but lead the good and noble to take you the more readily into the inner sanctuary of the heart.

"You will not mind my saying this. I have long wanted to tell you that I am not one of those fools who think that a service gabbled over a couple makes their children any better than the children of love.

"I hope you will not forget to write to

"Your very affectionate friend,

"Herbert Lovell."

A week later Charles got the following from Bianca di Caserta :—

"Dear Signor Carlo,

"I feel I must write to you, because we were good friends together, and it would not be friendship on my part if I were to be silent. I know that you love Euphrosyne, and Euphrosyne adores you, and to me it seems that you could not be better matched, and I love Euphrosyne so much that I am quite happy in seeing her happy, and therefore to see her sad makes me sad also, and she is sad now, and not without reason. The Baroness seems determined to marry her to my brother, and my brother is at present not unwilling, and has indeed broken off an engagement which he had contracted between himself and the Principessa di Benvenuta, of this town. They are not engaged yet, but it seems very imminent. I will still do my best to prevent this marriage, *for much as I love my brother, I love*—

(N.B.—Bianca scratched out the words I have underlined.) "Therefore be watchful, as I will be, and believe me ever yours,

"Bianca."

This letter rather upset Charles, but he trusted in Euphrosyne, and so made no mention of it to her. In a few days he took train to London, *viâ* Paris.

He had not left his hotel four days, when another note came from Bianca.

"Dear Charles,

"What I feared is done. Euphrosyne is affianced against her will to my brother.

"Bianca."

CHAPTER XX.

OPEN-EYED CONSPIRACY.

SCENE: A private room in one of the large hotels in the Strand.
TIME: Three o'clock in the afternoon of a rainy day.
PRESENT: Bartlemy Hiram, *alias* Dr. Toogood, *alias* Milwaukee Bartholomew.

"WHY does he not come?" said Bartlemy, consulting his watch with a gesture of great impatience. "What the deuce does he mean by keeping me waiting. We agreed to meet at two o'clock, and now it is past three. He is a good side too careless, is that Snorker, and by far too careless for me."

Then he began to pace up and down the room, muttering to himself—

"Why do I have dealings with this fellow—why? Because two heads are better than one, and four hands better than two, and punishment, when it falls on us, will fall divided, or perhaps, he! he! he! all on him. I seem especially exempt from that retribution which, as the world and poets, bah! say, is bound to come on crime. I am a criminal and I know it; but, the deuce, what is a man to do who wants to live and is too much of a gentleman to work, and who wants a gentleman's pleasures? Pleasure! Ah, I love thy name, sparkling wine, warm kisses, and the rattle of the dice, and are they not worth all the trouble they take to possess? But this *coup* which I am planning will free me for ever from the doubts of my position. It is true my wife's thousand a year is a resource, but she is damnably tight-fisted, and little is the benefit I get from it. To get it all and the other thing is now my object, and, as I cannot work it alone, I get this infernal Snorker to help me. I hold him tight, that is one comfort. Swindler at Monaco, forger at Marseilles, and blackleg in England, my knowledge of his history and his career gives me a tight grip on him, and he must serve me body and soul. He did that job with Esther well, and now she is out of the way matters are easier. Ha! I hear a step; it is my companion, my slave."

It was indeed Chizzlem, who, dripping wet, was ushered into the room by an obsequious waiter.

"Waiter," said Bartlemy, "two glasses of rum and water, bring the water and the bottle of rum; and now sir," said he, turning to Chizzlem, as soon as the waiter had gone out of the room, "why the d—l have you kept me waiting this time. You were to have been here an hour ago."

"I bet," said Snorker, "that when you hear what I have been doing, you will say my hour was well employed. Whom do you think I have seen in London?"

"Whom?"

"Charles Benson," said Snorker, triumphantly.

"Ha, where?"

"I first saw him in Fleet Street, looking into a bookseller's shop. I followed him down to Trafalgar Square, where he entered Morley's."

"Did you lose sight of him there?" asked Bartholomew.

"No, I entered into the hotel much against my will, you know I stayed there once, and was obliged to *déménager à la fiselle,* but I risked recognition, and went in and asked if Mr. Charles Hauberk were staying there."

"And they said?"

"Yes, he had just arrived. Didn't know if he was going to stay, had to clear out then, as I saw the proprietor in the hall, and couldn't trust my whiskers too far, you know."

"Yes, yes," said Bartholomew, "you did well. I could not afford to lose you just at present. Do you remember the old gentleman's address?"

"What, the old bloke whose ticker I scooted on board?"

"Yes, whom else?"

"I know his address."

"What is it?"

"Here is his card."

LUKE BENNETT,
17, Palgrave Square.

"And are you sure he believed that this Charles was the thief?"

"Certain, he kept slanging him all the way up to London."

"What did you do with the watch?"

"Dropped it for a fiver at a slop-shop at Southampton."

"Good; now what you have to do is to keep your eye on this Hauberk, or Benson."

"What for?"

"All in good time; I don't know whether to take you into my confidence or not. It is a grand *coup,* and will make our fortunes, but I have not grasped the whole matter yet, and don't want to spoil it by going to work too quick."

"Look here," said Chizzlem, irritably, "I don't call this square. All should be above board between pals, and I am blowed if I like to work in the dark. Some time ago you told me, 'I want Esther out of the way,' and I said 'Run her in as Polly,' and you agreed, and we had her put into a lunatic asylum, where she is now. Now you set me dodging this young man, and want to have him arrested. What is it all about? Come, be square, and at least let us know what's on the tappy."

Bartlemy kept silence, and, stirring his rum and water, seemed lost in thought. At last he said—

"Chizzlem, you're hard up, aren't you?"

"As hard up as a bloke who can't get a roafyanneps' worth of whisky on the slate can be."

"Well I am, too."

"Go on, you, with a wife worth twenty thousand pounds."

"Aye, which she keeps to herself, but, as I say, I am poor, and you are poor. We want money."

"Oh, no."

"And money must be had. How would a couple of thou. suit you?"

"That depends on what risk I have to run to get it. Bar the risk, amazingly well."

"Well, if you will help me you shall have it."

"What's the game?"

"Ah, that I won't tell you yet. I will tell you the first part, which we must do, we want funds to work the second."

"And the first part is"—

"To put my wife where Esther White is."

"That's what I advised you to do all along."

"Yes, and I mean to avail myself of your advice, and of your help now."

"And are the £2,000 for that?"

"Oh, no, that is the least part of it; the work comes afterwards."

"Well, tell us what it is, can't you," said Snorker impatiently.

Bartlemy looked at him, as if undecided what to say, then played with his spoon, took a gulp of rum and water, looked at Snorker again, drained his glass, and jumping to his feet started up, and, going up to Snorker, seized him by the arm and said—

"Step this way, I'll tell you all, and then see if it isn't worth our trouble."

So saying he drew him to the window, and for fully an hour the two men stood there discussing Bartlemy's plan, the gigantic daring and risks of which seemed to amuse, startle, and excite them by turn.

They spoke in whispers, but a listener at the

door might have caught the following disjointed words of Bartlemy's—

"*Lawyer—Grosvenor Gardens—Case for charity—Esther—Lord Hauberk— Wanted—Identity—Better terms—Man in possession—Keep others out of way—America.*"

"You are a clever fellow," said Chizzlem admiringly, as they returned from the window and once more took their places at the table. "A very clever fellow, Mil, and deserve to make your fortune, which you will do."

"Which I mean to do, and yours too."

"On a different scale, by Jove. I have not agreed to terms yet."

"I repeat my offer, £2,000 and no risk."

"I can't accept less than £4,000. You may throw in a little risk, if you like, for the money."

A wrangle then ensued between the two men as to the terms. Bartlemy reviled, threatened, cajoled and flattered his companion in turns, but Chizzlem would not give way. At last Bartlemy made the following proposal—

"A thousand pounds as soon as my wife's twenty are in my hands, and three thousand as soon as the other affair is settled. I won't budge an inch from this."

"Done with you," said Chizzlem; and they shook hands.

"Now the first thing to be done is to get your two medical friends down to Devonshire. Will they do the job on the same terms as they did Esther's business?" said Bartlemy.

"I think so. You'll pay all expenses, of course."

"Yes," said Bartlemy.

And here I must ask the reader who loves sensational incidents to excuse me if I refrain from entering into the details of the shameful proceeding which resulted in Sabine's confinement in a private lunatic asylum, and the custody of her property passing into the hands of her husband. The thing is done every day, and personally I know of several persons, chiefly helpless women, who are thus confined by their greedy, heartless relatives. In a short time the gloomy gates of Peckham Lodge had opened on another victim, and Sabine Hiram was as much dead to the world as if the tomb had closed over her.

The infamous practitioners who had given their certificates were well paid, and Snorker received his fee in the shape of five promissory notes of £200 each.

The next time the men met was a month later, the place was the same.

Hiram was there first, but Snorker did not long keep him waiting. As soon as he entered he said—

"Well, how was the thing done?"

"Capitally."

"And does this further plan No. 2?"

"Of course, I have money now my wife is out of the way. Esther is out of the way, and the field is clear."

"Ah, the chief person has escaped."

"How? What do you mean?"

"I was at Morley's again this morning. Charles Hauberk has left."

"When?"

"Yesterday."

"Where for?"

"I don't know."

"Did you ask?"

"How could I?"

"Well, he has gone, d—n him; we must find him, and sharp."

"Why?"

"Oh, hang you, Snorker, with all your questions. Don't you see that this matter must be pushed through sharp or others will reap the fruits? Look here, don't you see that others are already busy with this same matter? Have you not seen these two advertisements in the papers a hundred times?"

"The which?"

"These," said Bartlemy pointing to a newspaper that lay on the table; "there."

NOTICE.—Would the lady who helped a poor girl at the GROSVENOR HOTEL, in OCTOBER last, kindly communicate with the lawyer who called on her on that occasion? By doing so she will GREATLY oblige. Sister's address not known.

And lower down.

£500 REWARD.—Whoever can give information as to the whereabouts of ESTHER LOVELL, lately in America, and last seen in London, will receive the above reward. Also, should this meet the eye of ESTHER LOVELL, she is EARNESTLY entreated to COMMUNICATE with the advertiser at once.—John Bennett, Lincoln's Inn, London.

"What do you think a lawyer chap would offer £500 reward for were he not certain of making a lot of money? I guess he won't find Esther Lovell."

"Why not?" said Snorker, "suppose the Peckham Lodge people get hold of the paper."

"Well, and what then? you bet she don't get the papers to read; besides she don't call herself Lovell, but White."

"You're right," said Snorker. "What did you say the advertiser's name was?"

"Bennett, John George Bennett."

"Bennett? Why that's the name of the man of the watch."

"So it is. Bennett ain't a uncommon name."

"Well, but it is an odd coincidence, all the same. Let's look at the paper."

Bartlemy tossed the paper over to Snorker, who looked at the advertisements. Suddenly his attention was attracted, and he betrayed evident signs of excitement.

"What's up?" said Bartlemy. You are not thinking of going and blowing on the plant, are you? It would be £500 hardly earned if you did."

"Get out," said Snorker, indignantly. "Don't you know your pal better than that?"

"Then what's up?"

"Look here, another advertisement."

Snorker passed the paper to Bartlemy, pointing to this advertisement.

NOTICE.—CHARLES BENSON is requested to communicate with advertiser at once, when he will hear of something decidedly to his advantage.—J. G. BENNETT, Lincoln's Inn, London.

"Gad," said Bartlemy, "how could we let him go, when we might have him safe in quod."

"Had not we better let the matter slide?" said Chizzlem.

"Fool," said Bartlemy. "There are now a thousand reasons why we should not. It is no longer a question only of losing a fortune, but of our personal safety."

"How so?"

"How so? Bigamy, forgery, and other games we have played, will be exposed if this cursed Bennett finds out where Esther is."

"Who is this Bennett?"

"A barrister, who went to the bar from being a solicitor. He is an old man. I saw him at Grosvenor Gardens last year, when I was courting, pah! my wife. He came to talk about Esther Lovell. It appears that Miss Crosthwaite, my wife's sister, met Esther after I knocked her down, and took her to the Grosvenor, and there met Bennett. Luckily for us this Miss Crosthwaite, for reasons best known to herself hid Esther away down Westminster way, but gave my wife's address, and Bennett came to talk about matters. I shut him up before my wife, and had a private interview with him, then I learned what you know. I did not at the time care to occupy myself with the matter. I was too anxious to get Mrs. Hiram the Third safely married to me, or else I would have thought about it. Now that I am discontented with what I then thought a big fortune, I want to turn my knowledge to account, and make money. I did not want Bennett bothering about Esther, as I was afraid of betraying myself to this Sabine, so I told the servant to tell him we had gone away, which she did when he called again. What we have to do is this, to get to know where this Charles Benson is, and then go to work."

"Supposing I find he is in London, what then?"

"This is what you must do. Find his address, and then call on Luke Bennett at Palgrave Square, renew your acquaintance with him, and get him to come for a walk with you. Contrive to meet this Benson in your walk, point him out to Bennett as the man who stole his watch, get him arrested, and then trust to chance that he does not get off, but is kept quiet for a few weeks, till we have had time to act."

"But the matter will get into the papers; Bennett will find out where Charles is from the reports, even if his brother don't tell him. It seems to me the whole plot is worth nothing."

"Make all the objections you can," said Bartlemy. "You only help me, I want to know all the weak points. Go on."

"Well, here is another thing I have thought about. This Charles Benson must have friends, Miss Crosthwaite, for instance, friends at Oxford, and others who will answer the advertisement, and then where shall we be?"

"Benson alone is worth nothing to Bennett, who can do nothing and prove nothing without Esther. Why I want him out of the way is, to have the field all to myself. Were others to interfere, our chance would be worth nothing. Therefore, you must do as I said. Twenty to one Benson is in London, and left Morley's to go into lodgings."

"Well, if he is I will find him," said Snorker.

"Good-bye, then," said Bartholomew, rising; "go to your work."

"And you to yours."

"And I to mine," answered Bartholomew.

As soon as Snorker had gone Bartholomew rang the bell and bade the waiter bring him a peerage list and a file of the *Times* for the year 18—, and as there was no file kept, sent him round to a library in the Strand to borrow one.

When these came he set to work copying extracts and preparing a business-like document. He worked hard at this all the evening.

CHAPTER XXI.

THE MAN OF LAW.

DURING the month which had elapsed between the two interviews described in the former chapter, Mr. John Bennett had not been idle; and not discouraged by his want of success, still pursued his object with unremitting energy. From the advertisements which we have read we recognise his immediate object, namely, to find Esther Lovell and Charles Benson. Being a cautious man he had not as yet told anyone with what further object in view he was pursuing his search, but kept quiet and spent large sums of money in advertising. He wanted Esther, then, for some purpose of his own, and bitterly regretted having lost sight of her when by hazard he had met with her in London.

Mr. Bennett had in his youth been a solicitor, and had had some very good clients, but being taken very ill with brain fever, which bereft him for a long time of his memory, and paralyzed more or less his mental power, he had given up his practice. Finding, however, that he could not well live unconnected with things legal, he ate his dinners at Lincoln's Inn, and renting chambers there had started again as a barrister. Being very old when he was called he did not care to accept many briefs, but such as he did he worked out with very great care, and, generally, with success.

Recently, however, his head having become quite clear again, he seemed to be quite unsettled, and renouncing all practice set to work on a mysterious object which nobody could understand, but which he pursued with energy and application, which was quite wonderful in so old a gentleman.

On the morning of the day when Bartlemy had met Snorker, as described above, Mr. Bennett was sitting in his study reading his paper when his laundress knocked at his door and brought him two letters.

Mr. Bennett carefully perused the address ; they evidently came from people of the lower order, for one letter was addressed—

> MISTER JON GORGE BENNETT,
> Linkoln 'is In,
> London (*find 'im*).

and the other—

> JOHN GEORGE BENNED,
> Eskire Lincole inn
> london.

" News about Esther at last," cried the lawyer gladly, as he tore open the first letter and read—

"fishro tames strete.

"DEER SIR,

"I sees mi Pen to rite to yew, referang to Ester lovel, what yew advertize 4 in the Chronicle ofering 500£ reward for sich infermashon. She staid with me, ma, & grandma a long Time a-go, and left without setlin. Likewise she left a lokit, the which grandma Boned, but giv up to ma on heering of reward, the lokit yew can ave on paying er det, and Please to send the 500£ as I want to start a terbacker shop. With respecks in which I join

"VALINTINE, OR JACK, PIMMINS."

"P.S.—Yer not to set polis arter grandma what Boned the Lokit."

The lawyer smiled as he read the letter; and remarking, "Well, I hope the other letter will be more satisfactory," tore the second letter open. It ran as follows :—

"18, Burton Row, Westminster,
"London.

"SIR,

"I write in answer to your advertisement to say we ad a lady called Ester staid here for some time, what was wisited by a man what gave your name, and whom in 'er fewry attaking she chipped off a bit of the wallnut wood chare, which that aggravated my John that he could not enjoy his vittles, and had the bile when he diskivered it. Should this answer your rekirements please send the £500 by P.O.O., or in registered letter, or in stamps.

"To Yours Trewly,

"REBECCA MARTIN."

Whilst Mr. Bennett was taking a note of the address of each writer, and copying out the letters, a third letter was brought him. It came from Keswick.

"DEAR SIR,

"I am requested by Miss Dorothy Crosthwaite, who is ill in bed, to write to you with reference to your two advertisements.

"She bids me say that she placed Esther Lovell with a Miss Martin, at a house in Burton's Row, Westminster, the number of which she forgets.

"Charles Benson, or Hauberk as he calls himself, is abroad, and Miss Crosthwaite does not know his address.

"She expressed a hope that her conduct with reference to this unhappy woman did not really cause you great annoyance, and adds that she had given her word and could act in no other way.

"Believe me, Sir,

"Your obedient servant,

"MARY KENNEDY."

"It is clear I must see both Mr. Pimmins and Mrs. Martin," said the barrister drawing on his coat, and without delay he drove off to the Thames Street, and without much difficulty succeeded in finding Valentine's abode in Fish Row.

Mrs. Pimmins gave him all the information she

could about Esther, and readily gave up the locket when Mr. Bennett offered to pay the small debt which Esther had incurred. Valentine was not very pleased to hear that the lawyer did not think his information worth the £500, for ever since he had answered the letter he had done nothing but think of the tobacco shop he would open, and had indeed discounted a promise with his grandmother to supply her with unlimited snuff when his establishment was open by devouring that old lady's stock of peppermint drops.

The lawyer went next to Burton Row, and learned from Mrs. Martin that Esther had been with her, but that she had left without giving an address, information which Mrs. Martin thought fully worth £500, and who piteously remarked on hearing that Mr. Bennett was not prepared to pay the sum for it, "Wot am I terdo about the mangle I got on tick, 'oping yer would act the gentleman?"

Mr. Bennett could not say, and took his leave, remarking that if Mrs. Martin met Esther, and would inform him thereof, he would gladly pay her the worth of many mangles.

As soon as he got home, he examined the locket, the initials E. L. were entwined on the cover, and inside was the name of the maker.

"*J. Tyson, Jeweller, Melton Mowbray.*"

"That only proves what I already knew," said the lawyer, impatiently, "namely that this is the person I am seeking."

"Mrs. Martin's evidence was the most important.

Who can the Bennett be? Her description reminds me of someone that I have seen, who can it be? If my memory does not fail me now, I may make a grand discovery and be justified in paying for poor Mrs. Martin's mangle. By Jove, I've got it, it's the clergyman I saw at Grosvenor Gardens. I've got his card. James, bring me the Lovell file. There, the Rev. Bartlemy Hiram; now James, 'Clergy List,' quick, quick. D, E, F, G, H, Hi, Hir, Hirdon, hum, Higgings, Hickinbottom, hum, hum. Ah, here it is, Hirane. No, by Jove, there is no such name here. What a nuisance; wherever I turn I find difficulties. Well, I must be off now, dine with Brother Luke this evening."

With these words Mr. Bennett stepped out of his chambers, and made his way down Fleet Street towards Ludgate Hill. When he reached St. Paul's he suddenly remembered that he had that morning received a very pressing letter from a solicitor at Manchester, asking him if he could come down to that town to discuss a case which the solicitor wished to lay before him for his opinion, and which he could not do without Mr. Bennett's presence in Manchester.

He had quite forgotten the solicitor's letter, so anxious and preoccupied had he been with Esther's case, and not wishing to cause any delay, he stepped into a neighbouring post-office to telegraph his answer to Manchester.

Just as he entered the office, a man came running out and pushing against him violently muttered a hasty apology and ran down the street. Mr. Bennett had time to notice his appearance. He was a vulgar looking individual, dressed in a rather shabby blue serge suit, with a high hat, and an old red velvet tie. His face, which was covered with spots, was adorned with red whiskers, and dark red hair, and a very fiery nose.

Mr. Bennett passed into the office, and going to the counter where the telegraph forms lay, took one and began to write his address on it.

Suddenly he stopped and closely examined the form on which he was writing, then folding it up, put it into his pocket-book, hastily scribbled and sent off his telegram to Manchester on another form, and rushed out of the office, and, walking down the street as fast as he could, turned into the first refreshment shop he could see.

"Quick, a pen and paper!" he cried to the waiter, "and turn up the gas."

"What will the gentleman take?" said the waiter.

"Pen, ink, paper, and turn up the gas," shouted Bennett. Then, "Oh, anything else you like, half-a-half, or what is it."

"Half and half, yes, sir."

As soon as the gas was turned up, Mr. Bennett took the empty telegraph form out of his pocket-book and began eagerly to scan it.

Yes, sure enough, there, impressed in white letters on the form he had begun to use, was an exact copy of the telegram which the person who had occupied the telegraph counter just before him, had written on the form that had lain above it.

As soon as the ink came, Mr. Bennett began to fill in in black the indented letters, and when he had finished the telegram was reproduced in exactly the same hand as the original copy had been written in. It read thus:—

"*Dear Mil—Found Charles Benson; meet me at old place in an hour.*"

"That's very well," said Bennett, "but now for the address of the sender, and the sendee. Oh there, just my luck, I have got a clue and destroyed its utility myself." For Mr. Bennett, having filled in the parts of the form reserved for the addresser's name and address, the impress of the letters which had come through the form above was quite obliterated. Poor Mr. Bennett!

"Here," said the waiter, as the lawyer rushed out of the bar, "none of them games," and caught hold of him, "settle first, and then slope."

"(h, I beg pardon," said Mr. Bennett. "I am very much preoccupied and quite forgot it."

He was so vexed with himself, and with his unsuccessful attempts, that he could not go to his brother in the irritated temper he was in. So telegraphing to Luke not to expect him, he dined in a Fleet Street restaurant, and went home, thoroughly tired and dejected, to his chambers.

It was perhaps unfortunate that he did not, for Luke, after he had dined alone, received a visit from a gentleman who wished particularly to see him.

Luke, who felt dull and disappointed at having had to dine alone, allowed the visitor to be shown in, although the hour was a strange one for such a visit, and accordingly Mr. Chizzlem Snorker was ushered in.

"I have the pleasure of addressing Mr.?"— said Luke, rising.

"Chizzlem Snorker," said that gentleman.

"Mr. Snorker; hum, I beg pardon, but I really forget"—

"Oh no, you don't, sir," said Snorker, advancing and shaking his hand, "no, no, you don't. Don't you remember s.s. *Wolf*, plying between Southampton and Hamburg, (D.V.-ing, and weather permitting), and the beautiful watch, presented to you by his Grace the Duke of Northampton, which you lost?"

"Ah, I remember. Do you come to give me news of it? I shall be very grateful to you. Sit down please, and Charles, a glass and the port for this gentleman."

"Thank you," said Snorker. "No, I don't know where the watch is, but I know where the thief is, and his name."

"Do you," said Luke, "how very glad I am. That nasty young man, he pretended to be so swell. What's his name?"

"Legion," said Snorker, then lowering his voice, "his real name is 'Kedges.'"

"Kedges?"

"Yes, Bill Kedges. He calls himself Montmorency."

"And you know where he lives?"

"Aye, aye."

"I'll have him arrested."

"Of course."

"At once."

"No, no, wait till to-morrow at least. I'll help you, I'll go with you."

"Right you are."

"Says Moses, say, Mr. Bennett, what's got into your brother's head?"

"What brother?"

"John George."

"The barrister, how do you know he's my brother?"

"Can't I see the likeness; the same Romian nose, the same glad smile?"

"Go on, what do you mean about what's got into his head?"

"What's all these advertisements he's a putting into the papers."

"I don't know, how can I know?"

"Who's Esther Lovell?"

"I don't know. It's some case he's got hold of. He forgets he is no longer a solicitor."

"He was a solicitor, then?"

"Yes."

"Good practice?"

"Very, lots of lords, dukes, earls and barons on his books."

"Indeed."

"Yes, and it rather turned his head. Found his Brother Luke a cad, because Brother Luke went into the hardware trade."

"So, so got proud, did he?"

"As a duke. The attentions he got from Lord Brookshire for example, were enough to turn his head."

"Who's Lord Brookshire?"

"Dead, title extinct, present heir only got the barony. Right Honorable Lord Hauberk, of Carrickfergus, in Ireland."

"Then your brother was solicitor to Lord Hauberk, was he?"

"No, to Lord Brookshire."

"Same thing. Were they tight?"

"Very, he was quite a friend. Knew all Lord Brookshire's secrets. Tended my lord when my lord died; got a brain fever immediately afterwards, and lost his wits for several years. Not got them all back now. Strange and forgetful at times, but a damned good man of business all the same."

"Indeed. Well, sir, shall we go after Kedges to-morrow?"

"Nothing will suit me better. The scoundrel."

And after a warm shake of the hand, Mr. Chizzlem departed.

We must now go back to Mr. Charles *alias* Bill Kedges.

CHAPTER XXII.

OH, THAT MINE ENEMY WOULD WRITE A BOOK.

We left Charles at Venice, whence he had just departed for London when Bianca's note arrived announcing the engagement of Euphrosyne to Arnolfo Duke di Caserta.

Charles knew, therefore, nothing of this distressful incident, and as soon as he reached London, wrote the following letter, burning with love and full of tenderness, to his dear girl :—

"Morley's Hotel,
"London.

"My own Dear Euphrosyne,

"I cannot tell you how uneasy and distressed I have been, to have passed so many days before I could hear from you, for to me a day which brings me no letter from you is like a day on which the sun has never risen, and is to me one long, dark, dreary void, where fevered thoughts chase through my burning brain, and vague fears and anxieties give way, now to hope, now to stronger fear. I have just reached London, and I write to you the minute I have entered this hotel. I wrote to you on board the steamer from Naples, at Genoa, at Marseilles, at Lyons, and at Paris, to tell you of my progress. You will wonder what I have come to London for. Well, because I found myself idling in the south, wasting my time, and not advancing my project, and, to be near you —and yet so far away, was worse than to be really very far.

"How hateful London seems after the glorious south, and how ridiculously affected the people look contrasted with the children of nature I have left. Nobody seems to dress here in accordance with his position. Clerks with eighty pounds a year, go about like bookmakers just starting for the races; everybody seems to affect a sporting kind of dress, and men who never had, and never will have any connection with sporting matters, and who probably do not know a fox terrier from a folded blanket, or a full-bred horse from a park-hack, advertise their pretensions to be classed as gallant sportsmen the loudest. I am disgusted with London. What a wretched unit one feels amongst these millions. And yet, as I look out of my window on the thousands of people thronging, thronging, the square, rich and poor, old and young, in luxury, in rags, I think to myself that I envy not one of them, no, not the proud men rolling from their Clubs to the gilded halls of Westminster, for not one of them can ever know my happiness. Happiness? is that the word? for all I feel, all the delirious joy I experience when I think that you love me, and my heart throbs and my lips tingle at the remembrance of your kisses.

"Oh! why were we to be separated just when life seemed worth living? My pretty darling, write and tell me you love me, tell it me again, and again, I never shall weary of reading those words, and, when we meet, of hearing you say them.

"I am going to lose no time now, but will try and find work to do and make myself a position which will perhaps prove to your mother that Charles Hauberk has at least the noblest quality of an English gentleman—'pluck.' What that work will be, and what position I may hope to occupy, I cannot myself say. I mean tho' to try some literary work, and if I can earn enough thereby will go to the bar, and you know that in England the bar is the ladder to all honours.

"I take my MSS. to a publisher to-morrow; I shall try to get him to publish my poems and will send some of my roundabout sketches to the magazines. If these succeed I shall have reason to hope.

"We are both young, my Euphrosyne, and have time, but that time must not be long, for my heart is full unto bursting with yearning after you.

"Write soon, my dear girl, to your devoted and loving

"CHARLES HAUBERK."

In accordance with his statement he sent a line to De Clyner and Co., referring to his poems.

The same evening he received the following note from those publishers:—

"DEAR SIR,

"In answer to your note of to-day we beg to say that the chances against our being able to publish your volume of poems are so great, that we will not even ask you to send your MSS. for inspection.

"Yours truly,

"De Clyner and Co."

Other publishers, to whom he applied, thanked him for his kind offer, which, however, they were obliged to decline, as they had for the present completed their arrangements; others, in view of the present want of popularity of poetry, would be glad to see the MSS. if Mr. C. Hauberk wished to publish the poems at his own expense, but could take no risk themselves; others suggested the feasibility of publishing them on the half-profit system, which, as Charles was worldly-wise enough to know, means all the expense and no gain, &c., &c.

Luckily Charles was not quite dependent on his work for living, for having paid all his debts, he had still an annuity of £100 to live on, but was by no means inclined to remain in this state of golden mediocrity of purse, and set to work with unabashed vigour to find employment. At last, he saw an advertisement in the *Clapham Mercury*, where it was announced that the editor wanted the services of an active young man to write leaderettes, reviews, &c., and applying at the office in Manor Street, engaged with the *Clapham Mercury*, to contribute daily at the rate of 30s. a week. In order to be near the office of this mighty organ, Charles moved from Trafalgar Square to Manor Street, where he took a small lodging and occupied himself with his new work, giving great satisfaction to his employer.

A great trouble to him, however, was the silence of Euphrosyne. The whole time he had been in London, he had not received a single line from her; and though at first he attributed this silence to the probability of the Bienaimée family having gone to their *villegiatura*, as time went on and no news came, he grew very anxious, and kept writing in turn to Bianca, and Euphrosyne, imploring for news.

It was on the second day of his stay at Manor Street and, having been busy all the afternoon correcting proofs for the paper, he was sitting listlessly in his room, watching through the open window the antics of a monkey, dancing to the music of a squeaky barrel organ which was being ground by an Italian. Charles, who had a warm sympathy for all the children of the paese del Si, leant out of the window, and engaging the man's good graces by throwing him a sixpenny bit, asked him in Italian—

"From what part of Italy are you?"

"Firenze, Signor."

"Florence is beautiful, is it not?"

"As beautiful as your sposa will be, Excellency."

"Ah!" said Charles, thinking of Euphrosyne.

"Do you know the Duca di Caserta by name?"

"Il buon Duca?"

"Yes."

"Si, Signore. He is going to be married."

"Veramente, to whom?" said Charles turning pale.

"To the Principessa di Benvenuta."

"Are you sure?"

"Certainly."

"When did you leave Florence?"

"Three months ago."

"Ah, thank you?"

The Italian saluted, and went on his way grinding forth the tune from the *Traviata*—

Ai nostri montagni
Ritorneremo.

"So," said Charles, "di Caserta is to be married, nay, probably is married by this time. I have nothing to fear then."

To him thus musing then entered his landlady, a kind old soul. Said she—

"Look here, sir, I don't like to see a young man sit cooped up all day, it ain't good for you, you know. I have a son myself, who is as good a lad as lad can be, and works hard, but he do like a bit of life. Why don't you go out on to the 'Igh Street and see a bit of life? all Clapham is out just now."

Charles smiled, thinking to himself the world will only give you credit for what you appear to be; perhaps, however, in this case the credit given is creditable.

However, he was not unwilling to take the

woman's advice, and went out to take a walk. Skirting the gay throng of drapers' assistants, grocers' factotums, and milliners' apprentices, who formed the "life" of Clapham, he walked out on to the common, and when he was tired sat down to smoke on a bench, watching the smoke rings as they curled upwards into the air, and thinking of Italy, of Herbert, of his love.

A man who had been loitering near passed and repassed him, turning his head towards him each time. His behaviour attracted Charles's notice, and looking at the man he seemed to himself to recognize a face he had seen before. Surely he had seen that blue serge suit when it was newer and fresher, and that red velvet tie before it had lost its ruddy splendour, that pimpled face, that fiery nose, those carrot whiskers and dark red hair; where had he seen them? While thus reflecting the man, who had taken a long stare at him, suddenly ran away at full speed, and the last Charles saw of him was his getting into a cab at the outskirts of the Common.

"It seems to me," said Charles as he walked home, "that I have seen that man somewhere, and under some unfavourable circumstances," but for the life of him he could not remember where or when.

When he got home he found a lot of work awaiting him; amongst others there was a book of poems to review. He opened it and smiled as he read the title—

CHERRY BLOSSOMS AND WILL-O'-THE-WISPS.

BEING THE EARLY POEMS OF

JAMES MANGLES-PEEBLES-MANGLES,

Of St. Mar. Coll., Oxon.

(Published at the Author's own expense.)

"Now I can have my revenge," cried Charles, seizing his pen, "my enemy has written a book."

CHAPTER XXIII.

PECKHAM LODGE.

The reader will of course bear in mind that the events referring to Snorker, Hiram, Bennett, and Charles, related in the three last chapters, all took place on the same day in different parts of the town. Thus while Charles was cutting up his former friend's book of poems, Bennett was fuming in his chambers over the piece of evidence he had with his own hand destroyed, Snorker, Hiram, and the unconscious Luke Bennett were plotting against our hero.

I must now beg my reader to come with me to another part of the town, and bear in mind that the events to be related in this chapter take place on the same day as the above.

In a small back street in South Kensington, shut in all round by high walls, stood a mysterious-looking house, known to the world as Peckham Lodge, a private lunatic asylum.

It was here that both victims of the villanous Hiram were confined. Esther in the poor ward and Sabine in the ward of Class 3, for the kind Bartlemy felt he could not do less for his dear wife than pay £40 a year to Dr. Phillipot for her sustenance.

Well, all this day Sabine had been trying to make her case public, and, by drawing attention to the foul conspiracy of which she was a victim, procure her release. To give the reader an insight into this unfortunate lady's real state of mind I have determined to give copies of certain letters which she contrived to write at odd intervals since her confinement. By bribing a female attendant she had managed to get the wherewithal to write.

Out of a heap of letters which have come into my hands I will give two or three.

(LETTER No. 1.)

"*To the Right Honourable William Ewart Gladstone, 73, Harley Street.*

"Peckham Lodge,
"South Kensington.

"SIR,

"Having seen a great deal in the newspapers about our lunacy laws, I write to you, as a member of Parliament, to request you to interest yourself in the matter, for I, as a victim, can assure you that newspapers do not nearly come up to the truth in the descriptions of asylums; numbers of persons like myself are incarcerated in these places who are perfectly in their senses, and those who are insane are not properly treated. The animals are better off, for if I were to go down a street and see a horse or a dog ill-used I should certainly give the person in charge; but here I can do nothing, for were I to interfere I should only bring down upon myself vengeance without doing any good. There is no prosecuting for assault or getting at the common law of the country, as the postage of letters is prevented.

"The Commissioners themselves allow that these places are often used as reformatories, and think it quite right if any good is done. But how can any good be learned when violence, dirt, and disorderly conduct of every description is the order of the day, and from thence, of course, they get to calumniating persons, and thrust them here under false certificates.

"If Drs. were punished with the utmost rigour of the law who give false certificates;

"If madhouse-keepers had their licences taken from them and their houses shut up when rational beings are found in them, without entering into any why or because;

"If pillar letter-boxes were by act of Parliament placed over the grounds, the postman himself taking the letters as is done in the streets, and the places policed, these evils might in a manner be remedied.

"The limits of my paper will not admit of my going into this matter as fully as I wish, or going into my own case; sufficient it is to say that I have applied over and over again to the Commissioners to be set at liberty without effect, and I have no other means of redress.

"I would not mind anyone seeing the copies of the letters I have sent to the Commissioners.

"Trusting you will excuse deficiencies, I am, sir, yours respectfully,

(*Not sent.*) "SABINE HIRAM."

(Letter No. 2.)

"*To the Reverend the Incumbent of the Keswick Parish Church.*

"Rev. Sir,

"Would you kindly use your influence with my sister, Miss Dorothy Crosthwaite, to come and take me out of this place, as a relation can, as let the party be insane or not, and I think it would be better not to enter into any questions on that head until I am once fairly out of this asylum.

"I have written several letters to her, but fear they have not been posted, and she would do well to claim them.

"I cannot extricate myself, for they all so play into each others hands that it is impossible to do anything; and every effort I make to free myself only makes my position the more intolerable. I believe that the Drs. have been writing to her, but I fear they do not wish to put me in my right position, that of having been brought to an asylum at all, but to go on a leave of absence, as they call it, tie up my property from me, and perhaps eventually bring me to this place again. This I must protest against with all the means in my power; I have been dreadfully calumniated by someone or other to the Commissioners, and that they are not the use I expected them to be of to me, and I wish to be as I was before, my own mistress, and soon.

"If my sister only knew the base and even dangerous things that have been said of her by those whom she has befriended she would at once see that her best plan was to make friends with me.

"I am, reverend sir, respectfully,

(*Not sent.*) "SABINE HIRAM."

(LETTER No. 3.)

"*To the Rev. Bartlemy Hiram, Honeymoon Cottage, Rosedale, Devonshire.*

"DEAR BARTLEMY,

"I have written many times to you to tell you where I am and how shamefully I am treated, and you do not, as a husband ought, answer my letters or take the necessary steps to free me from this place.

"When I was dragged away from my home I told the men that I should inform you of their conduct, but they only laughed and did not care. I have been several weeks in this odious place, and never have heard from you. Why don't you write? and why don't you look after your wife?

"I tried to escape the other day out of an attic window, but was caught by Dr. Phillipot, and the same evening was stripped by two female warders and beaten, and left to sleep on the bare boards without a covering.

"I am quite sane, and you know it; my brain fever at Paris has not altered that, and you know it too; but if I am left here much longer, and treated as I am being treated now, I shall certainly go mad, and then what will become of me!

"So please make arrangements to come and take me out. If you apply to the Commissioners at 19,

Whitehall Place, and say you are a clergyman, and tell them of that book your ancestor wrote, I think they will entertain your application.

"I hope you are not interfering with my property, it was settled on me, you know. I expect to find a nice sum when I come out, as the interest must have accumulated.

"I advise you to turn your thoughts to suitable employment, and alter your behaviour.

"I remain, your wife,

"SABINE HIRAM."

(*Not sent.*)

In noting some of the peculiarities of the style, the reader must, in justice to the unhappy woman, before forming an opinion, remember the intense anxieties caused by her position, her suffering, and the brain fever from which she had only so recently recovered.

She had never met Esther, who, as has been stated, was confined in the poor ward of Peckham House. Esther, it is true, presented some excuse for her confinement, for her afflictions since she first left her home, the shame, suffering, and disgrace which had come upon her in London, her exposure to the inclemencies of the weather and the pangs of hunger, her fear and hatred of Bartholomew, had all worked perniciously on her mind, which had always been most excitable. For reasons which will afterwards appear, she wished to be hiding, and as her absolute poverty prevented her from finding any suitable asylum for herself, she had fallen an almost willing victim to the machinations of the villanous Snorker.

It was late. Sabine was sitting in the wretched room assigned to her in an attic of Peckham Lodge. Ostensibly she was sewing, repairing a dress of hers, but in reality she was furtively penning another letter. She held the ink between her knees, and wrote hastily at intervals on a sheet of paper which lay in the drawer of the table.

It was one of many letters she had written to the Commissioners in Lunacy which had never been posted. A tallow candle was burning in the window-sill, and flickered in the draught. Outside, the wind was soughing in the trees, and whistling mournfully in the eaves. Sabine was writing, and very intent on her work. Suddenly she looked up, a shadow had fallen athwart the table and intercepted the light. With beating heart and straining eyes she rose and screamed for help. For there at the window. stood a tall figure draped in black, looking outwards, the same fearful apparition she had beheld at the Clarendon Hotel at Dover.

"Who are you? Whence did you come? What do you want?" she cried, advancing towards the door.

"I am Esther Lovell. I come from below. It is you I want, Mrs. Hiram," answered the figure turning, and revealing not the grinning face of a skull, but a beautiful face of a woman worn and weary, and afflicted even unto death.

"Stay," she continued, for Sabine, who had by

no means recovered from her fright, was going away. "Stay," she repeated gently, "I mean you no harm. I am only a poor woman, like yourself, only perhaps more miserable."

"You startled me," said Sabine, looking with evident fear on her strange visitor. I had a bad dream once. The night I married"—

"Bartlemy Hiram."

"Ha, you know his name?"

"I have reason to, I am his wife."

"Wife?" screamed Sabine. "A lie, a lie, it is I, it is I who am Mrs. Hiram."

"No more than I am."

"What do you mean? I married him legally."

"And I legally; he was married before ever you, poor woman, met him. His name is not Hiram at all, it is Bartholomew."

"Oh, oh, oh!"

"I heard below," continued Esther, "that a person called Hiram was staying here. I overheard two female warders speaking about you; I heard them say what a shame it was you were confined here. They said you were as sane as they were."

"They only spoke the truth," said Sabine, and added with a little sniff, "and a little saner, I hope."

"As soon as I heard this I knew who you were. Oh, I knew that another victim had fallen to the devilry of that wretch. I used to hate you, I cursed you. I thought of you as a young woman. I did not expect to see grey hairs."

"Indeed," said Sabine tartly, "and pray where do you see grey hairs?"

"I do not mean to offend you. I rather take your part. No, do not think I mean to be rude. You are a victim of his, as I am."

"How do you mean a victim? My husband has surely nothing to do with my being here. I fancy poor Bartie is in the greatest distress, and would rush to free me if he only knew where I am."

"Poor Bartie knows that well enough," said Esther. "The same doctors that brought you here brought me here too."

"That proves nothing."

"It proves everything. Those doctors were hired by a wretch, an accomplice of your husband, I know it well."

"How did you, if you knew the plot, allow yourself to come here?"

"I came here willingly."

"Willingly? to this place?"

"Aye, right willingly. I want a hiding place. I am being looked for."

"By the police, young woman?"—

"No, not by the police. By a lawyer."

"You don't mean to say you are the woman whom my idiotic sister helped at the Grosvenor Hotel last year?"

"I was helped last year in sore distress, but she who helped me was an angel from heaven."

"An angel indeed! That's the first time I have heard Dorothy Crosthwaite called an angel."

"Dorothy? Dorothy?" said Esther musing. "I like that name, It was my baby girl's." Then aloud, "Yes, an angel of heaven. Then you are her sister? I thought I remembered the face. There is a difference, it is true."

"A difference—I hope so."

"She had a sweet face, and there was something touching in seeing so childlike a smile on her wrinkled lips."

"Wrinkled, yes, yes, she has wrinkles."

"You do not love your sister, I see," said Esther, "she merits your love, I am sure."

"She is a big fool. She is always doing odd things; she ought to come here a little. I am sure it would do her good. She was jealous of my marriage, and for all the nonsense you have said about dear Bartie, I believe it was she who got me brought here. She wanted to get married herself, to a mere boy, a Charles Bensberk or Hawson, or some name like that. She loved him."

"Say that again, say that again," said Esther, excitedly.

"Aye, I will. She loved a lad, a chance child, called Charles Benson, ah! yes, that's it."

"She loved him?"

"Yes, like an old fool."

"She loved him?"

"Yes."

"Then," said Esther, with infinite sweetness, "the time has come when I can show Dorothy that I am not ungrateful. Good-bye, Mrs. Hiram. There will be a stir in this accursed house to-night." And so saying, she gathered her cloak round her, and ran swiftly out of the room. A letter, which had been in her pocket, fell to the ground. Apparently she did not notice it, but ran on and left it lying on the floor.

Sabine saw it fall, and picked it up. Taking it to the light she read the address—

"To Mrs. Esther White,
"Poor Ward,
"Peckham Lodge,
"Cenasue Street,
"South Kensington."

"I'll read it," she said. "Mrs. Hiram, indeed."

And taking the letter from the envelope, she read as follows:—

"My Angel Girl,

"I tell you I loves you, y? be so crewel to me, and treet my eart with disdane. I got you run in and will get you run out. I 8 Bartlemy, and 8 all his jobs. Y? can't you love me as I loves you and I would elp you to get your revinge onim. We are doing a Big Job this time. We've got scent of a lawyer's job, and shall make a pile. I get £2000. With this we 2 could be happy. We are going to arest a bloke called Charles Benson, al i ass Orberk, and I'm on his track

This done we are sure of the Pile. If you want to get out from the Pollies

"Send a smile,
"From above
"Full of love,
"on your devoted dove.
"CHIZZLEM SNORKER."

Sabine had only just finished reading this curious epistle when Esther darted in again. Seeing the letter in Sabine's possession she rushed forward, and snatching it out of her hand, darted away again as quickly as she had come.

That night there was a stir at Peckham Lodge. A patient who, on account of her tranquillity and general good behaviour, had been allowed larger liberties than the others, had escaped from the house.

That patient was Esther White.

END OF VOL. II.

www.ingramcontent.com/pod-product-compliance
Lightning Source LLC
Chambersburg PA
CBHW030807020726
47499CB00006B/1797

* 9 7 8 3 3 3 7 0 4 6 1 0 1 *